- THE TRAP -

Sarah Wray lives in Belfast with her husband and three children. She has a degree in Genetics from Queen's University Belfast, has worked as a research scientist, a child-minder and a science teacher, and has done voluntary work with disabled children. Her first children's novel, *The Forbidden Room*, beat thousands of other entries to win the nationwide Wow Factor competition.

You can read more about Sarah at her website:

www.sarahwray.com

Praise for *The Forbidden Room*:

'There is a clever mystery at the heart of this novel, but what is best about it is the understanding, unsentimental portrayal of the disabled heroine.' *Observer*

'Atmospheric and tense . . . Full of issues and excitement, *The Forbidden Room* will be devoured by readers aged 12 plus.' *School Librarian*

THE TRAP

Sarah Wray

To Alison

Best wishes
from
Sarah Wray

ff

faber and faber

First published in 2008
by Faber and Faber Limited
3 Queen Square London WC1N 3AU

Typeset by Faber and Faber Limited
Printed in England by CPI BookMarque, Croydon

A CIP record for this book
is available from the British Library

ISBN 978-0-571-23921-4

2 4 6 8 10 9 7 5 3 1

*For Sheila, Gill, Maureen,
Irene, Patricia, Karen and Arlene –
my book group buddies!*

- *Prologue* -
IN THE DARK

I'm running for my life. I can't see a thing. It's terrifying, but I have to keep moving, to get to a safe place, if a safe place even exists. The darkness is so intense that it literally makes no difference whether my eyes are open or closed. My throat feels dry and sore because I'm panting and gasping for air. The sound of my ragged breathing, as well as the slap of my feet on the stone, is echoing off the rocks above and beneath and on either side of me. The noise is making my mind play tricks. I think I hear animals chasing me, hungry slavering beasts closing in on me. I can almost hear the weight of the earth, threatening to collapse on top of me. I'm so scared that my fear is like a physical presence, grabbing me and squeezing me until the tightness is unbearable.

I can't run any farther. I'm so disorientated anyway that for all I know I could be running towards danger now, not away from it – not to mention the threat of running blindly off the edge of a cliff, or into a crack that will trap me for ever. I feel sick and dizzy. The lack of oxygen and the low blood-sugar telling me to rest are competing

I

with the flood of adrenalin that's urging me to keep moving. I feel like a feather tossed about in a hurricane.

I sink to my knees and cradle my face in my hands. My palms feel wet and sticky and I can smell the iron in the blood from my hands and from my face. I was flailing my arms about as a substitute for eyes as I ran, so the rocky walls of the cave have torn them ruthlessly. While I was running, I couldn't feel my hands, but since I've stopped they've begun to throb with pain, to go with the pain in my head. I wonder if I'm injured anywhere else. I can't even think clearly enough to tell. I feel confused and woozy, like I'm losing consciousness. It's a nice feeling. Nicer than reality. I'm lying in a gently rocking cradle falling deeper and deeper . . . NO! I must stay awake. To go to sleep would be the end of everything. I'm not ready to die deep underground thousands of miles away from home.

Stand up.

Walk.

Think.

My body obeys reluctantly, stumbling forward, cursing me for not letting me rest.

Keep walking.

Stay awake.

Think.

I don't want to think. I want to let go.

Tell yourself the story. How did you get here? Remember? The day the letter from America came. Could that boy who waited so eagerly, so happily for that letter really be me?

part one

The Camp

- One -
WRYP

It was a Saturday in May. It's an effort to make myself remember, but once I do, the blackness in my mind is chased away for a while by the flood of images that the memory brings. The postman had to ring the doorbell because the letter was too big to go through the letter-box. My big brother Ryan assumed it was for him – another university prospectus. 'Out the way, butt breath,' he said, shoving past me as I opened the front door, then, 'Oh looky – Lukie got a letter. Does it make you feel all grown up, Lukie? Maybe it's that "how-to-stop-being-such-an-annoying-nerdy-geek" correspondence course you've been waiting for. Quick, take it; you need all the help you can get.' I gave him a withering look and snatched the package from him, trying not to show how excited I was about it. The first rule of survival with my brother Ryan is not to show any sign of weakness.

I knew what it was before I opened it. I spotted the letters 'WRYP' printed on the top left corner of the envelope. Well Rounded Youth Program. I know it sounds like a fat camp, but it's not – it's a camp for smart kids, academic achievers. It's American. Some well-meaning American had this idea that smart kids find it difficult to integrate socially. The old lonely nerd caricature. And that we're all rubbish at sport, or basically anything non-academic, so they set up this programme where smart kids from Britain and America get together at camp and learn how to be more normal. My maths teacher, Mr Platt, put me forward for it. I had to sit this sort of IQ test, and fill in forms and stuff way back in January, and then when I'd pretty much given up hope, I got a phone call telling me I was in. Two months in New York State. Woohoo!

I took the letter up to my room. When I say 'my room', I mean the room I've shared with Ryan all my life. I've been counting off the months until he goes away to university so I can finally get some privacy. I wonder now if I'll ever see it again. It would be ironic if I died just when I was about to get the room to myself.

I sat on my bed and opened the envelope.

There was a colour brochure as well as some letters and more forms. I ignored the letters to begin with, and picked up the brochure. The front cover had in its centre a picture of a big log-cabin-like structure with the words 'Camp Hope Welcomes You' carved above its main door. Around the cabin was a montage of pictures of happy, fit-looking teenagers engaged in activities like archery, abseiling, canoeing, and hiking – lots of healthy out-doorsy stuff. I couldn't help feeling a surge of excitement: I was going to America for two months! I couldn't believe it.

*

It was six weeks after the Camp Hope bumf arrived that I left home.

The night before, I packed and repacked my bag about ten times, making sure I'd got everything: torch and spare batteries, insulin, blood-testing kits, mosquito repellent, camera, sun-cream, swimming trunks, pens, paper, clothes . . . etc etc. Ryan thought it was hilarious.

I went over my travel plans about a hundred times in my head – not that it was likely that I'd forget them: taxi to the railway station, train to London Paddington, then change to the Heathrow Express, then meet up with the WRYP reps at the airport in Terminal Three for the Virgin Atlantic flight to New York JFK. I was ridiculously nervous. I told myself to stop being such a wimp – you're almost sixteen, for crying out loud, not some little kid who's never been anywhere. All right, so I'd never been further than the bus into town without a parent or a teacher being there, but, I told myself, you're practically a man now, you can do this.

In the morning a taxi came to take me to the railway station. Then I had to endure the hugs and tears as my parents saw me into the taxi, and Ryan's cry of 'Good riddance, loser', which was the last thing I heard before slamming the door. My dad paid the taxi driver in advance, which made me cringe with embarrassment, although I was secretly relieved that I didn't have to worry about sorting that out. In the railway station, though, I was left to fend for myself – a man alone in the world.

The train journey was pretty straightforward: I found the platforms for the train to Paddington, and then the Heathrow Express easily enough. In the airport I spotted a couple more red WRYP stickers on the luggage of kids heading towards a lift to the departures area, so I followed them. Immediately as the lift opened on Terminal Three, I saw lots more kids all with the now-familiar red stickers huddled around a couple of adults. The adults were wearing sweatshirts emblazoned with the WRYP logo, and one of them was carrying a red flag on a pole. Blasts of air from the air-conditioning unit in the ceiling were making the flag dance and I wondered if the WRYP rep was going to check it into the hold, or bring it on to the plane as hand luggage.

'Muffin tops,' said a boy behind me. I looked around to see who he was talking to, and realised it was me. 'See those two girls?' I followed his pointed finger to a group of girls; I wasn't sure which two he was referring to. 'Look,' he went on, 'see how their jeans are really tight and low cut – it makes their flesh bulge out over the top of their jeans like the top of a muffin. Not a good look. Still, they have got nice jugs.'

'Oh yeah,' I said vaguely, letting my gaze roam over the girls' figures, then blushing when one of them caught my eye.

'I'm Matt, by the way,' said the boy. 'Matt Newbury.'

I should have looked at him and introduced myself, but my eyes were still drawn to the group of girls.

'Hey,' Matt said, noticing where I was looking, 'stop staring – they'll think you're some kind of perve.'

I wasn't staring at the girls with the tight jeans and nice jugs, though – it was someone else. Another of the girls, standing beside them and looking hugely different and yet exactly the same as when I'd last seen her, more than five years ago. Ignoring Matt, I walked towards her, trying to decide if it really was her, although I didn't actually have any doubt.

'Natalie!'

She looked at me, with her head on one side, as if she was weighing up the chances of me being who she thought I was.

'Luke?'

'Yeah, it's me – Luke Sheldon, from Hawthorn Street. I haven't seen you since . . . I mean, in years. You look, wow, you look great.'

Natalie and I had been friends in junior school. Our headmaster, Mr Kenyan, had selected the children who showed the most potential intellectually to go to weekly meetings in his office. He would play word games with us or just discuss things like history or current affairs. Natalie and I were both in Mr Kenyan's special class and we consoled each other in whispered conversations about how going to it always meant missing PE. Once he asked us to get into pairs and then set us a task to design a device to weigh an elephant. The boy beside me, an annoying boy called James Parker who was always picking his nose, looked like he was about to ask to be my partner, so before he could, I quickly asked Natalie – she beamed at me like I'd just given her a million pounds or something. The friendship kind of developed from there.

We got on really well – we were always at each other's house. We used to play spies and send each other coded messages. We took it really seriously – if the enemy ever infiltrated St Peter's Primary School we'd be ready for them.

She moved away before we moved up to secondary school. Her mum and dad were in an accident. Her dad had restored an old fishing boat, and one day he and her mum were out in the boat and they never came back. Missing presumed dead. Natalie went and lived with her aunt and uncle, and I hadn't seen her since then.

I noticed then that the other girls had all stopped their chatting and were watching the exchange between me and Natalie as if it was a scene from the latest soap opera.

'Luke! You're going to Camp Hope? Wow, what a coincidence.'

She looked me up and down, smiling in disbelief. 'You look, um, tall.'

'Yeah,' I laughed, wishing now that I'd waited until most of the girls had gone on one of their mass trips to the toilet before going and speaking to Natalie. 'I had, you know, a growth spurt.'

She nodded, and then her eyes looked past me. 'Who's your friend?'

Matt had sidled up beside me, and stood looking handsome and taking the attention of the girls that moments ago I had wanted to be off me.

'Um, this is Matt. Matt Newbury, meet Natalie Anderson. We used to be best friends when we were little – we haven't seen each other in years.'

'Hey,' said Matt, 'best friends. Cool.'

He put out his hand to shake Natalie's, and held it just a moment longer than was necessary before letting go. She smiled at him, and I noticed that the braces that she'd worn on her teeth back when we were ten had done a good job.

- Two -
LOG CABINS IN THE WOODS

One of the WRYP reps came over then to talk to me about bringing my insulin meds on to the plane. I went off with him to see to the paperwork. By the time I got back, all the hold luggage had been checked in and I joined the others in the queue to go through security.

The metal-detector siren blared as I stepped through, and I realised that I hadn't removed the injector pen from my pocket. I took it out and showed it to the security woman, who had been one of the ones to go over my meds with me earlier, so she smiled and waved me through.

In the departure lounge, Natalie came and sat on a chair beside mine.

'Luke,' Natalie said, 'how long have you been diabetic? I never knew you were.'

'It was not long after you went away,' I said. 'I'd just turned eleven.'

I remember being told what was wrong with me. Just about the worst news for an eleven-year-old boy: sweets could kill me. And for the rest of my life injections were going to happen every day. I'd cried and shouted and begged and pleaded, but nobody would change their minds and make it go away.

'What happened? I mean, how did they find out that you had it? Did you like go into a coma or something?'

I couldn't help blushing when she asked me that – I'd have liked to be able to tell her something cool like, 'No, I just got injured rescuing this baby from a burning building, and one of the routine hospital tests showed up the diabetes.' Ideas like that always come to me after the event, though, and at the time all I could think to say was, 'Er, no, they just, y'know, did some tests and that was that.' I didn't tell her that my first symptoms were a wild case of crotch-itch, accompanied by the need to pee copiously every five minutes. Some things are best left unsaid.

The rep with the flag stood up then and started giving us a talk about behaving on the plane. Her accent was American, and sounded strange amidst all the English voices. She said the seating had been assigned so that everyone sat with the people they would be sharing a cabin with at camp. She started going around the room with a clipboard and boarding passes. It turned out that the boy Matt was in my cabin, as well as four other boys. The rep told us to get to know our cabin mates, so Natalie went off to meet the girls she'd be sharing with. Matt and I introduced ourselves to the other boys: Jack Slater, Arash Ashouri, Mark Blackwell, and an Irish boy called Eoin Flynn. Jack looked nervous but friendly, Arash told me that my name was an anagram of 'nuked hellos', and Eoin seemed all right too – except that he had already formed a friendship with Mark Blackwell, who instantly reminded me of Ryan. They didn't look alike, but when Mark reacted to my friendly greeting with a scowl and a sarcastic comment it was like he'd been possessed by my brother and sent to annoy me. God must have a sense of humour, I thought. Thankfully Mark and Eoin were a few seats away from me on the plane.

The take-off was cool – like a roller-coaster climbing a hill, except really fast, as fast as if it was falling down the steepest slope in reverse. The flight was pretty long and boring. There were TV screens in the backs of the seats in front of us, with channels of movies or music or sitcoms that you could flick through. My headphones didn't work properly, though. I told the stewardess, and she brought me a new set, which were possibly even worse, so I gave up.

After a while, the stewards asked people to close their shutters and everyone gradually fell asleep. At one point I woke up and lifted the shutter just a little to peek out. What I saw out of the window was amazing. We were flying over a snowy, rocky place that was dazzlingly bright. I'm sure we were pretty high, but it looked like you could step out of the plane right on to one of the sparkling white peaks. There were white ridges as far as I could see. And it looked so – I don't know, so clean and unspoilt. It was like someone had solidified pure light and whipped it up into peaks – it hurt my eyes to look at it.

The stewardess came and asked me to close the shutter. As soon as it was shut I had to ask myself if I really did see what I thought I did. Maybe there was nothing but ocean out there and I dreamt up the incandescent landscape. Even now I'm not sure if it was real or not.

When the plane landed it felt like the end of a really long day, but because of the time difference it was only early afternoon. The plane didn't connect with a walkway, so we got to walk down steps right on to the runway in the open air and stand on American soil (well, tarmac) right away. It was really hot and bright and totally weird. I could hardly get my head around actually being thousands of miles away from anywhere I'd ever been before.

It took ages getting our bags, and then waiting for everyone to go through customs. The airport was filled with the sound of American voices, which made our accents sound strange even to my ears. Then we all trooped outside where a coach was waiting to drive us up north to the Adirondack Mountains – the home of Camp Hope.

I had that dry-eyed, surreal feeling after napping on the plane and waking up at totally the wrong time of day. I think everyone did, as people were yawning and rubbing their eyes everywhere I looked. No one slept on the coach, though. We were a bunch of wide-eyed kids staring at the backdrop we'd seen a thousand times on TV shows and movies, but never in real life. The ragged skyline of New York City – shining skyscrapers standing like monoliths, with the pointed peak of the

Empire State Building towering over them all, sharp against the clear blue sky that looked somehow different from the blue sky back home. We even stared at the people in the other cars – real live Americans.

We drove over bridges, past sleepy suburbs with houses that really did look like the homes of the Disney Channel families – with white wooden gables and painted shutters and even porch swings and tree-houses and mailboxes with raised flags at the ends of wide driveways. Then the road just kept on going – past fields and forests interspersed with diners and motels flashing neon signs advertising swimming pools and bed massagers, and past endless fast-food outlets: Denny's and Wendy's and McDonald's and Taco Bell, or Sizzler's Steak and Seafood Specials, one of which we stopped at for dinner. I was struck by how enormous America really is. The trip from the airport to the camp seemed like hardly any distance when you looked at the map of the whole USA, and yet it took ages. I bet you could drive the length of Great Britain in the time it took to get to the top of New York State.

The last few miles were along a lane that tunnelled through a forest of spruce and birch trees. Occasionally through gaps in the trees mountains could be seen, their peaks looking almost purple in the hazy evening sunshine. As the trees closed in around us, glimpses of the mountains became rarer. Branches scraped along the sides of the bus, and in the gloom under the treetops' shadow it felt like we could be lost in Hansel and Gretel's wood with the witch's cottage just around the corner. Twice I saw something move in the woods – something big enough to rustle branches and send birds flying upwards. I remembered how America has bears and wolves and even mountain lions still living wild, and felt a shudder of excitement.

When the bus came out of the woods, it was like the sun coming out from behind the clouds, and we blinked in the light, our eyes slowly focusing. We had arrived at Camp Hope.

A driveway lined with whitewashed rocks led to the central building: a large, dark wooden cabin with a stone chimney at one end and windows along the sides. It was raised off the ground on wooden stilts with steps leading up to double doors. Just like in the picture in the brochure, an archway above its doors bore the carved inscription: 'Camp Hope Welcomes You'.

This main cabin was flanked by smaller buildings, all made predominantly of the same dark wood, and I noticed some of the signs that hung above their doors: 'Art Store' or 'Supplies'. A little way off to the left and the right I could make out clusters of individual cabins, nestled in the shade of leafy trees, which would be where we slept while we were at camp. Twinkling in the distance I could see the edge of a lake, with a wooden pier and jetty, and shelves of colourful kayaks showing themselves alluringly through the open door of a boat-house.

The driveway was flanked with yellowing grass and areas fenced off for different activities. I could see archery targets off to my right, beside a shed that must have stored arrows and bows, and other fenced-off areas whose purposes weren't immediately obvious. On the left, as well as a corral with stables, there was a large circle of fat logs lying on their sides like benches around a smaller circle of rocks. Within the rocky circle wood was piled like a tepee in preparation for a bonfire, and the little boy inside me couldn't wait to see the flames dancing.

Matt was looking out of the windows too, and nodding in appreciation of what he saw. 'See that big building there?' he said, pointing at a kind of barn behind the main cabin.

'Yeah.'

'Well, if those are the boys' cabins –' He pointed to the cabins on the left. '– and those are the girls' –' He pointed to the other set of cabins. '– I bet if you can get behind that barn, it would give you great cover to get to the girls' cabins after lights out.'

He grinned at me and winked, and I wasn't sure if he was serious or not. I've never been one for doing things that might get me into trouble, but something about Matt made me feel daring. Like why shouldn't I live it up a little? What harm could it do?

'Cool,' I said, as if there had been no internal debate and sneaking into the girls' cabins after dark had been my plan all along. 'We could put toads in their beds.'

Matt choked on a snigger and rolled his eyes at me. 'You want to go into the girls' cabins so you can play practical jokes? You have a lot to learn, my son.'

I turned away, stung and embarrassed. Matt didn't

even seem to notice that I was annoyed. As the bus pulled up outside the main cabin, he said in a corny cowboy accent, 'Grab your bag, partner, we're here.'

We all clambered off the bus, stiff and tired and excited, and watched our luggage being piled up beside the bus by the driver. A warm breeze, heavy with humidity and smelling like pine air-freshener, flapped our dishevelled clothes and lifted dry dirt off the ground in brown clouds. Some people, all wearing the same red camp T-shirts and white shorts, came out of the main cabin and walked, smiling, towards us. The leader was an older man who looked just like William Shatner, that guy who used to be Captain Kirk in *Star Trek*. Beside him was a female version of himself, who smiled at us as if she was ravenous and we were a freshly prepared feast. They were flanked by a rag-tag collection of younger adults, most of whom looked to be aged between eighteen and twenty-five. I wondered what they were doing there. I mean, I knew they were the 'camp counsellors', our teachers (or babysitters) while we are at camp, but what made them want to be there? Although for some it looked like a vocation – open, genuine, warm smiles said, 'I'm here for you, buddy' – others scowled or looked bored, and I wondered if they could have been forced to come here, for community service, or to get college credit, or something like that.

William Shatner introduced himself as Captain Bud, and the woman beside him as his wife Doris. He droned on for a bit about how Camp Hope was one big happy family. We stood listening, fidgeting and shifting our weight from foot to foot – still, it felt good to be standing in the fresh air after sitting for hours on the bus and I was glad that the welcome was not happening inside the cabin. When Captain Bud was finished, the young counsellors started calling out the names of the kids in their charge, and shepherding their little flocks off to their individual cabins. I watched with sadness while the female counsellors led the girls away to the cabins on the right. Of course I didn't think us boys would get female cabin counsellors, but I had allowed myself to indulge in a tiny spark of hope.

I was looking away when my name was called, and when my head whipped back, I saw that the guy *in loco parentis* for me and Matt and the four other boys looked like he was one small step away from the chain gang. His fine blond hair was longer than that of the other male counsellors, who all looked very clean-cut, and his chin had the kind of rough stubble that you could light matches off. His expression was anything but open and warm. If any of the counsellors were here as punishment for violent crime, it surely had to be him. I smiled at the other boys (except Mark) as we retrieved our bags from the pile beside the bus, but none of us spoke as we followed our counsellor. He introduced himself as 'Drew'. His accent was the slow drawl of the southern United States and he reminded me of Cletus the slack-jawed yokel from *The Simpsons*.

He pointed out the toilets and shower block on the way, then climbed the two steps up to the door of our cabin, which was labelled 'Chipmunks', and swung it open. 'This way, gentlemen,' he said. 'Welcome to the Camp Hope Savoy.'

Our first look at the inside of the cabin showed a basic wooden structure with rough rafters and no windows. Six sets of bunks lined the walls. When we walked in, we could see that one was obviously already occupied, with Drew's belongings stacked on the bottom bunk and his sleeping bag laid out on the top. Matt and I headed for the bunks furthest from Drew's, but Mark and Eoin beat us to it. I caught Mark's eye as he hauled his bag on to the top bunk. He stopped with his heavy bag half-way up, but showed no sign of discomfort at holding it there. He stared at me, his lip curled into a snarl as if he was silently daring me to challenge him. Rather than have a stand-off, Matt and I retreated and took bunks to the left of the door. Mark smirked after us, as if to say we were too easy. I thought I heard the word 'pansies' muttered behind our backs, but I chose to ignore it.

I felt cheated by there being a bully at Camp Hope. At school it always seemed to be the thick kids that filled that role – I didn't think I'd have to deal with thuggish behaviour at a camp for smart kids. I guess I hadn't figured on the evil genius type.

There were cupboards beside each bunk, and the beams in the walls provided niches to put things in like torches or books in. As we unpacked a few things, Drew sprawled on his bunk watching us.

'I have to tell you boys,' he said, his voice cutting through the clatter of our unpacking with quiet force, 'that for us all to be happy here at Camp Hope, you have to follow the rules. There are camp rules and there are *my* rules – you understand me?'

Not sure whether to respond, we didn't, until he repeated the question, and we murmured yeses.

'Some of the rules of camp I don't consider to be all that important, and I will therefore turn a blind eye if any of you should agree with my assessment and choose to flout them. However . . .' He shouted this word, and I jumped and fumbled a can of mosquito spray that clattered loudly to the floor. 'However, my rules are gospel, and you will obey them. Got it?'

More mumbled yeses.

'I shall advise you of my rules presently,' Drew went on. 'Right now, though, we are required to join the other happy campers for initiation. Follow me.'

Leaving the unpacking half-finished, we followed Drew out of the cabin. Matt and I caught each other's eye and pulled faces behind Drew's back.

More groups of boys were coming out of the other cabins, which were also labelled with the names of various woodland creatures. Some of the counsellors were chatting happily to the boys from their cabins. Why didn't I get one of them as my counsellor? I asked myself. Why does fate have it in for me?

Initiation was taking place at the bonfire that I'd seen as we drove up the driveway. Chairs had been arranged around the log benches to accommodate us all and the logs and the first rows of chairs had already been taken by the girls. The fire looked like it had just been lit: flames crackled through the kindling at the base of the fire, but the branches making up the tepee still caged it – black lines like prison bars against its glow. It was growing dark, and the warmth that had been in the air earlier was leaching away. I filed with the other boys into chairs, now three rows back from the fire, and strained to feel its heat. As the last of the boys took their seats, I watched the fire. Flames suddenly leapt up, engulfing their prison bars and turning them into ferocious energy. Above the fire black specks of ash and soot carelessly floated upwards and away on the wind.

The chattering that had filled the smoky air stopped suddenly and I lowered my gaze from the top of the fire to see Captain Bud rising like a tribal god from the heart of the inferno. Actually he just stood up from behind the fire and stepped on to a platform to address us, but the effect was pretty spectacular. All eyes fixed on him as we waited for him to speak.

'Well, let me repeat the welcome I offered earlier,' he began, smiling at us from his lofty position. 'We are so happy to have you Brits here in the glorious US of A. We love our country, and sharing what we love is our gift to the world. From the splendour of the mountains to the . . .'

I have to admit that my mind wandered at this point. Pretty early into Captain Bud's speech I know, but I found his self-congratulatory tone annoying and didn't really want to hear his love poem to America, so instead I tuned him out and listened to the other sounds. A constant noise that I hadn't noticed begin but which now filled the air was the shrill, rhythmical chirruping of insects. Were they grasshoppers? Or cicadas? Over that sound I occasionally heard a whinny or a nose-snorting, lip-blowing noise that must have been made by the horses in the nearby stables. The fire crackled, and sometimes popped loudly, spewing orange embers that quickly turned black away from the nurturing heat of the flames. I could even just make out tiny lapping noises from the lake, or at least imagined I could. I picked up the odd word as Captain Bud rambled on, something about a spiritual journey of self-discovery and allowing nature to guide you to wholeness. People around me were yawning. I couldn't make out the time on my watch in the gloom, but allowing for the hours added to our day, our body clocks must have been way into tomorrow. Everyone started shuffling and standing up, and since I hadn't heard what Captain Bud had just said, I looked at Matt questioningly.

'Food,' he said. 'This way.'

Cool.

The main cabin was used as the dining hall. Inside it was like a giant version of the sleeping cabins, except with tables and chairs instead of beds. There was a huge fireplace at one end, in which a fire almost as spectacular as the bonfire blazed merrily. There was a serving hatch in the corner, connected with the kitchens on the other side, and a long staff table beside it. We were told by Drew to sit with him around a smaller table which we didn't quite fill, and he chose Matt and me to collect food for our table from the hatch.

Supper was chicken soup with something called

cornbread, which looked like sponge cake, but tasted savoury and was actually pretty good. We had to drink milk with supper, which was weird – I hadn't drunk a glass of milk since I was about five – and the soup was followed up with chocolate chip cookies.

I ate a little of my cookie, and then gave the rest of it to Matt, so as not to send my blood glucose levels too high. Mark-The-Evil-Genius said something to his lap-dog Eoin and they both sniggered. Drew looked at them. 'What's the joke?' he said. 'Share it with the rest of us, boys.'

'Oh, it's nothing,' he said. 'I just thought it's sweet the way Luke gave his biscuit to Matt – they must be *really* good friends.'

'Drop dead, Ev –' I was about to call him Evil Genius, and had to make myself remember that his name is Mark. 'Drop dead, Mark,' I said. 'I can't eat too much sugar because I'm diabetic – not that that's any of your business.'

'Oh, I'm so sorry,' he said, sounding anything but sorry. 'I thought you were just a nice person.'

Jack and Arash at least were interested in my diabetes, and started asking me the usual questions – do I have to inject myself, would it kill me if I ate a big choccy bar, stuff like that. I showed them the injector pen which I always carry with me and they were suitably impressed. While I did, Matt gathered up the plates and took them back to the hatch.

After supper the other staff members introduced themselves: the guy in charge of the riding stables, the camp nurse, the lifeguard for the lake, the climbing instructor . . . Again, I didn't pay much attention. Matt and I were flicking stray chocolate chips at each other and thinking it was much funnier than it really was. One thing that I picked up on was that the American campers would be arriving the next afternoon. That's why there are extra bunks in the cabin, and empty seats at our table, I thought. Cool.

We were all like walking zombies after supper, we were so tired, and even the strangeness of being in a sleeping bag on a bunk in a log cabin in the woods of north New York State couldn't keep me awake.

- Three -
THE LAW OF THE JUNGLE

We were woken up that first morning at camp by a real live bugle call. The strangled sound of the trumpet added to the surreal feeling of waking up somewhere unfamiliar, and several tousle-headed boys sat up sharply and looked around in confusion.

'Wakey wakey, rise and shine,' said Drew as we stumbled out of our bunks. 'Hurry off to the shower block, boys – you don't want to be late for breakfast.'

The shower block was a confusing crush of sleepy teenage boys, but we eventually made it clean and fresh to breakfast, which was porridge, followed by a run-down of the day's schedule with Drew, who had a printout for each of us.

My activities on the first day were: hiking, fire-building, horse-riding, and archery. With my timetable I was given a map of the camp, with crosses marking where I had to go for different activities. Matt was on the same schedule as me, but those of the other boys varied slightly.

We had some free time before the first activity, so I

went off by myself to do my blood sugar test. I sat on a tree-stump beside the lake – I wanted to find somewhere secluded to inject myself and I thought my spot by the lake was perfect.

There was a tiny lizard standing on a rock beside where I sat, its right foreleg raised, poised for action. It was about fifteen centimetres long from head to tail, and bright orange – the colour of an orange highlighter pen. I wished I had my camera to photograph the little creature. It was so unlike anything I'd ever seen before. All of a sudden it seemed to realise it was being watched, though, and scurried off.

I must have sat there for longer than I thought, because I looked at my watch and saw it was time for the first activity. I quickly stowed my insulin in the cabin before heading off to the hiking shed.

I was so excited and happy. The summer stretched out before me full of potential – I had no idea that Camp Hope would offer me anything but harmless fun.

When I arrived, Matt was already at the hiking shed talking to Natalie. Natalie seemed flustered when I said hello, and I thought with bitterness that I must have interrupted something between her and Matt. I pointedly turned away from them and said hello to Ashley, a blonde girl from Natalie's cabin. Ashley proved to be shy, and hard work to talk to, but I acted like we were having the best time ever.

The girl teaching hiking was one of the American counsellors, Arleen. She had long, lean, tanned legs and shiny brown hair and a genuine enthusiasm which was contagious. We spent most of the time going over the contents of the hiking bags stored in the hiking shed: whistles to blow in an emergency, water canteens that have to be filled before every hike, bags for trail mix (which is kind of like dry muesli with nuts and raisins and stuff that you get to nibble on hikes – yummy, I don't think), laminated maps of the area around the camp, and finally compasses to find your way home if you get lost. Then Arleen took us to the edge of the woods and showed us the path leading to the beginning of all the hiking trails, where different coloured arrows were painted on trees to mark the various routes that we would be following over the summer.

We saw some chipmunks scurrying about in the trees and Arleen said they are quite tame and will come into the cabins to steal any candy that's left lying around – cool.

After hiking we had fifteen minutes to get to fire-building. I started telling Matt and Natalie and Ashley about the orange lizard I'd seen earlier. I didn't see Mark and Eoin coming up behind us.

'Those lizards are all over the place, you freaking moron,' Mark said from over my shoulder. 'I guess you're just too lovesick looking at pretty boy Matt to notice them.'

Before I had time to think of a scathing enough response to this, he went on, 'You think the orange is cool? Wait until you see the colours that come out of them when you smush them with a rock.'

I looked at him, horrified, and he laughed back at

me, making squelching noises. Eoin at least had the decency to say, 'Mark, that's disgusting – what have the poor wee lizards ever done to you?'

Mark looked at his buddy with mock sympathy. 'Oh, I'm sorry,' he said. 'Have I upset you? Maybe you'd like to join the other girls here and make a lizard hospital?' Eoin looked for a moment like he might take him up on the offer and ditch him for us, but after a couple of heartbeats, he said, 'What, these losers? I don't think so.' And the two of them broke away from us and made their own way to the fire-building area.

Drew was teaching fire-building. He had a tiny tepee fire lit, and we sat around it as he went through a laminated flip-book describing the differences between kindling and timber and fuel, and various types of bonfires.

'Listen up, boys and girls,' Drew drawled, putting the book down and idly whittling a thick twig with a knife he'd drawn from his jeans pocket. 'Youse all might be book-smart, which is all well and good for passing exams and getting high-paid jobs an' all, but this is the real world. The law of the jungle. Man versus nature. Man versus beast, man versus man.' He waved his knife to punctuate these statements and the light from his demonstration fire glinted against the blade. 'See, the fundamental difference between man and beast is fire,' he said. 'We can create it, we can control it, we can use it. But like everything else in this world it comes with a price.

'Fire is wild,' he said, leaning in towards the little blazing tepee. 'It's dangerous. It could kill you.' He thrust his knife forward as he said 'kill', making everyone gasp and move backwards. 'Or maim you.' This time he swept his knife in an arc, as if he was itching to demonstrate some maiming of his own. He grinned, obviously enjoying the effect his knife-waving was having on us. 'So what do you need to think about before lighting a fire?'

There was silence following his question – we were all still a bit stunned by his talk of death and maiming.

'What, cat got your tongues?'

'Um, you need to think about how to put the fire out?' one of the girls said.

'Give that girl a cookie!' Drew said, lifting the flip-book again.

He turned over a new page in the book, showing how you have to clear a space in the dirt and circle it with rocks before building a fire in the middle. 'First you need to trap it,' he said, 'and then, when the time is right, you need to be able to kill it.' He slammed his knife point-first into the twig he'd been whittling, and left it protruding from the wood, swaying slightly. Then he indicated a row of metal buckets behind him. 'You will be building your fires in groups of four,' he said, suddenly all businesslike. 'I want you to allocate one person to fill the bucket with water from the lake and bring it back, one to make a clear circle ringed with stones, one to gather kindling, and the other to gather timber.'

Matt and I turned to Natalie and Ashley and we all agreed to work together. My job was to make a clearing in the ground for the fire. I used my fingers to brush away fallen pine needles and twigs and small pebbles.

Something caught on my fingernail and bent it back painfully. 'Yeow!' I yelled, putting my finger in my mouth and sucking it before realising it was filthy from scrabbling about in the dirt. I looked at what had caught my fingernail and saw something shiny and white buried in the soil. I started to dig it out with a twig, while Drew ambled over to me. 'You hurt yourself, Luke?' he asked.

'Oh no, I just bent my fingernail on this.'

I showed him the white object, which had just broken loose from the dirt.

'Woo, looky here,' he said. 'You just found yourself a bear tooth. Big one too. Leave it with me, I'll bore a hole in it – you should wear it around your neck. Good-luck charm.'

By the time the others returned I had the clearing ready, and I told them about the bear tooth. 'Cool,' said Matt.

Ashley looked worried, and broke her usual silence to say, 'Are there bears in these woods, do you think? Do they come into the camp?'

Mark Blackwell must spend his whole life eavesdropping on other people's conversations, because he came over at that point and said, 'I saw a programme about bears. They never used to attack humans, but now because of losing their habitat, and climate change and all that, they're really desperate, and have started getting over their fear of people, and stealing our food and stuff. And some of them get the taste for us, and start attacking humans just for the fun of it. And, d'you know what, they found out on this programme that bears prefer attacking blonde females – something to do with the way they . . .' He paused and wrinkled his nose before saying the last word: '. . . smell.'

Ashley looked even paler than usual. 'Ignore him,' I said to her. 'He's making it up. Bears going after blonde females! Does he think we're stupid?'

Mark pretended to ponder this question while he walked back to Eoin and the two other boys they were working with. He said something to them and they all looked over to us and laughed. I turned my back to them and started trying to balance twigs against each other in a tepee shape. It was actually harder than it looked, and by the time Drew told us to clear up, we hadn't managed to build our fire successfully. Mark's of course was crackling happily and I was sorely tempted to kick it in his face.

After fire-building we had lunch, and it was after lunch that the camp stopped being just about having fun and meeting people, and became much more sinister. Because that's when we found the first clue.

We had half an hour's free time before horse-riding, so Matt and I went to the cabin to get some more mosquito repellent before going for a wander around the camp. We were the first ones back to the cabin, and when we pushed open the door, something white flapped up in the breeze and then fluttered back to the ground. I picked it up and looked at it – it was a note, except it didn't make any sense:

```
AR ZNE TJOX XN RAOG XMK

XHKJCEHK, ZNE MJFK XN RNWWNT

XMK PWEKC — NH KWCK!
```

I stared at the note, and then passed it to Matt, who stared at it too.

'What, is it Russian or something?' Matt said.

'No, it's not Russian,' I said, wondering for a moment if Matt got into camp for his looks rather than his brain. 'Russian is written with the Cyrillic alphabet. This is not anything – I mean, not any language – it's a code.'

Someone was coming up the steps to the cabin, and I'm not sure why, but I quickly hid the coded message in the pocket of my jeans. It was only Jack and Arash. They told us they'd been kayaking, and how cool it was, except that their knees hurt from kneeling in the boats. We told them about hiking and fire-building, but neither of us mentioned the note.

'Who's it from, d'you think?' I asked Matt, as we walked towards the stables a little later.

'Who's it from? We don't even know who it's to,' he said. 'It's probably set up by the camp, you know, to test if our brains are really as good as they're supposed to be. It did say in the brochure that there would be a prize for problem solving.'

'Yeah,' I said, thoughtfully. 'Everyone would have one then – every cabin, I mean.'

'Well, they probably do,' Matt said.

The smell from the stables hung in the hot air like an

invisible fog. We instantly slowed our pace when it hit us, and noticed that others were also waving the air away from their noses and making disgusted noises. Big buzzing flies hovered around the dung heap that lay between us and the open gate to the corral, and like kids running past an imaginary sleeping monster, we braved the stench and hurried on through. I saw Natalie leaning against the wooden fence and quickened my pace so as to reach her before Matt.

'Did you get a note in your cabin?' I asked her.

'A note? No. Why, did you send me one?'

Stupidly I blushed when she asked that, and said, 'No, but I, we . . .' As Matt caught up, I added, 'We got one. Look, it's coded.'

I took the now-crumpled note out of my pocket and showed it to Natalie and Ashley, who also leaned in to have a look.

'It's a substitution cipher,' Natalie said, after studying it for a couple of minutes. 'Like the ones we used to make. Do you remember? When we were kids?'

'Yeah,' I said. I knew that by sharing childhood memories we were excluding Matt and Ashley from the conversation, but I couldn't help preening and adding, 'Do you remember that time we made cipher wheels to code messages and Miss Almond caught us passing notes in class and got so cross because she couldn't work out what they meant?'

Natalie and I had made cipher wheels by each making two circles, one smaller than the other, with the letters of the alphabet written around the edges in different orders.

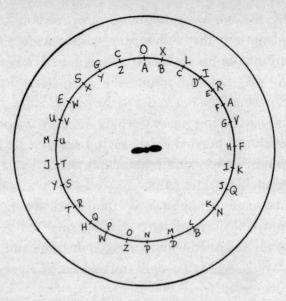

We attached the two wheels together with a clip so that they could both be turned around. Because we both had the same two wheels, we could code messages by setting the wheels to a certain position, and reading off the letters from the other wheel. Obviously Matt didn't know what we were talking about. He made feeble attempts to talk to Ashley, but I could see his eyes flicking to us rather than paying attention to her. Unfortunately the riding instructor showed up then, so we had to leave our code-breaking until later and instead learn the parts of the saddle and bridle, and the theory of how to climb on to a horse.

The girls weren't doing archery with us, so they went off somewhere else after horse-riding. Matt was sulky, probably still annoyed about me and Natalie reminiscing about our past, and started showing off to some other boys and doing impressions of the bow-legged guy who taught horse-riding. I ignored him and made my way over to the archery field, hoping that we would actually get to fire some arrows.

It looked like I was going to be disappointed, as we spent a lot of time being told what everything was called. Finally the instructor, a tall bearded man called Dave, said, 'Okay, time to have some fun. Everybody select a bow that reaches from the ground to your shoulder, and that you can comfortably lift, and five arrows, and go and stand behind the shooting line.' He showed us how to hold the bow and draw the string, and how to release the arrows, and then told us the safety rules, which were pretty obvious – like don't shoot at anyone, and don't go in front of someone else who is shooting. And then it was time to try firing at the targets.

I stood with my bow drawn and an arrow poised, quivering with potential energy, and imagined I was a hunter. I could see my prey, a huge lumbering mammoth. It had spotted me, and had turned towards me. It was me or it; everything depended on my arrow flying true – whether I would bring home food for my family, or whether nothing would be brought to them but my broken body. I could feel my blood pulsing through my veins and my adrenalin rising . . .

'Hey, Robin Hood, where's your merry men?'

The arrow twanged from my bow, wobbled, and dropped to the ground only a couple of feet from where I stood. I turned, startled, to see who had spoken, almost choking on my sharp intake of breath.

It was a girl. The light caught her honey-coloured hair and made a halo glow around her. She stood almost as tall as me, but without any of my gawkiness. An amused smile played on her full lips and her hazel eyes danced, taking me in and then resting back to gaze into mine. I got the impression that she had a great body, but since I couldn't tear my eyes away from her face, I really couldn't say for sure.

'Hello?' she said, her voice surprisingly deep for a girl, and as sexy as only an American voice can be.

'Ug,' I said.

'Well, hello, Ug,' she said. 'I'm Kathryn Star Hernandez. You may call me Star.'

I explained hurriedly that my name was not Ug but Luke, and she told me that she'd snuck away from the welcome lecture that Captain Bud was giving and was reacquainting herself with the old place.

'You've been here before?' I asked. She ignored my question and instead told me that she loved my accent and asked me if all British boys were so thin. I blushed and told her that I was thinner than most, and she said it made me look Dickensian, like Oliver Twist. Not sure what to make of that, I just said, 'Oh.'

I didn't get time to shoot any more, as Dave told everyone to down their bows and retrieve their arrows, then pack everything away back in the store. Star said she'd better get back to the others before she was missed, so she was gone by the time I met up with Matt.

'Did you see my shots?' he asked happily. 'Four out of

the five hit the target and one was almost a bull's-eye. Dave says I'm a natural. How did you do?'

I thought of my one pathetic arrow, but I didn't care. 'Great!' I said. 'I think I'm a natural too.'

After I met Star, all thoughts of the clue in my pocket had flown from my mind. I wish I could go back to how things were then. I wish the clue had stayed in my pocket. I wish we'd never translated it and got drawn into the series of events that followed.

- Four -
CIPHER PARTY

The American campers were officially introduced at dinner, with Star amongst them. She sought me out with her eyes, and smiled at me like we were old friends. Matt didn't seem to notice, and I really wanted to say, 'Look at that hot girl smiling at me – she said I look Dickensian,' but I didn't want to have to explain in front of everyone, so I bit my tongue. Four boys joined our table: Marco, Tyler, Zachary, and KC. One of them, I think it was Tyler, said, 'Hey, British dudes – awesome.' There was some staring at each other as if we were all specimens at the zoo or something. I guess we were waiting for them to do something 'American' and they were waiting for us to do something 'British'. In the meantime, we ate dinner, and conversation was stilted.

After dinner there was free time, and everyone stayed around the dining hall after the food was cleared away. Natalie and Ashley came over to us and asked to see the note again. I reluctantly took it out in front of the other guys at the table, and of course everyone wanted to know what it was all about.

'A coded message – neat,' said Marco, who was kind of fat, but good-humoured; one of those people who keep everyone else laughing.

'Hey, show it to me,' said Arash. 'I've been British junior Scrabble champion two years in a row.'

'Oh gosh, Arash, how interesting,' said Mark, dripping sarcasm. 'You might not be able to break the code, but at least you could tell us how many points it would score on a triple.'

'Ho, ho, ho,' Arash shot back. 'Very funny. The point is, I think about words and letters and all that, so when I look at this code, I see that there are lots of letter Ks, which makes me think that it probably stands for E, because E is the most commonly used letter in the English language.'

'Hey, good work, Sherlock,' said Marco. 'And the second most common letter in the code is X, right, which would make it what?'

'T, gentlemen?' The voice was unmistakable. I whirled around in my chair, almost knocking it over in the process. Natalie made an exaggerated throat-clearing noise, and Star turned to her and said, 'Sorry – and ladies.'

'Star,' I said, 'hi.'

'Is this a private cipher party, or can anyone join in?'

I hurriedly moved over to make space for Star, crashing my chair into Jack's in the process. 'Hey!' he said, but I hardly heard him. I was already leaning over to pull up chairs for Star and a second girl who was following her.

'So, is this like a parlour game?' Star asked. 'Shall we play charades next?'

Matt answered her: 'We found this mysterious coded message in our cabin. We're trying to figure it out.'

Star turned away from Matt and back to me, and said, 'Cool. Has anyone got a pen? Let's solve this baby.'

Natalie fished a pen from somewhere in her clothes, and pulled the paper over to herself. She started writing Es under all the places where the letter K was in the message, and then she wrote Ts under the letter Xs.

'Hey, where'd the Ts come from?' Marco asked.

Natalie answered him: 'As, um, Star correctly pointed out, T is the second most frequent letter in the English language.'

'Oh!' said Marco, 'I thought she meant tea, as in what English people drink.' He laughed heartily, but Natalie didn't even smile – she was frowning in concentration over the paper.

'M must stand for H,' she said, 'which would make those two three-letter words "the".' She filled in the Hs and then pushed the page into the middle of the table for everyone to see.

AR ZNE TJOX XN RAOG XMK
          T   T   THE

XHKJCEHK, ZNE MJFK XN RNWWNT
T E   E,   H E   T

XMK PWEKC — NH KWCK!
THE   E   —   E   E!

'Hey, look,' said Star. 'The two-letter word "XN" is in the message twice, which is T something, which has to be the word "to", so N must equal O.' Star flicked her fingers in Natalie's direction, to indicate that she wanted the pen. Natalie handed it over, and Star filled in the letter Os.

'Now,' said Arash, 'there's a two-letter word that starts with O, which could be "of", or "on", or "or".'

KC, one of the American boys who hadn't really said much yet, piped in with 'If you look at that word "XHKJCEHK", H follows X in it. So if X equals T, then H can't be F or N – so it has to be R, right?'

'Right!' Natalie grabbed the paper and pen back from Star, and wrote in the three letter Rs. Now the message looked like this:

```
AR  ZNE  TJOX  XN  RAOG  XMK
    O         T   TO        THE

XHKJCEHK,  ZNE  MJFK  XN  RNWWNT
TRE    RE,   O    H E  TO  O    O

XMK  PWEKC  —  NH  KWCK !
THE   E     —  OR   E  E!
```

'Oh!' Star sounded excited. 'I bet that word is "treasure" on the second row. Fill it in . . .'

'Natalie.'

'Hi, Natalie – pleased to make your acquaintance. I'm Kathryn Star Hernandez, but everyone calls me Star.'

'So I've heard,' said Natalie under her breath, but loud enough that I heard her at least. She filled in the letters anyway:

```
AR  ZNE  TJOX  XN  RAOG  XMK
    OU     A  T  TO        THE
XHKJCEHK,  ZNE  MJFK  XN  RNWWNT
TREASURE,   OU  HA E  TO   O   O
XMK  PWEKC  —  NH  KWCK !
THE  UES  —  OR  E SE !
```

Probable words leapt out at us now, and even Mark looked interested. Before long the code was broken, and the message read:

IF YOU WANT TO FIND THE
TREASURE, YOU HAVE TO FOLLOW
THE CLUES – OR ELSE!

The buzz of excitement around the table only intensified once the message was solved. What treasure? What clues? Who could have written the note, and what did they mean by 'or else'?

Speculation came thick and fast. Matt repeated his theory that it was set up by the camp leaders, and that the treasure was probably some dumb educational thing, or having your name added to the list of camp heroes or something lame like that.

'No way, man,' said Marco. 'There's bound to be real treasure hidden somewhere around here. I mean, there're caves and forests with hardly any people about – perfect hiding place for ill-gotten gains, right?'

'Yeah,' said Mark, 'because if I was a criminal, with treasure hidden in them thar hills, the first thing I would do would be to send clues to a bunch of teenage kids so they could find it and steal it from me.

What, are you all morons?'

We tried to ignore Mark, but he did have a point. Why would someone send us clues to find their treasure?

'Maybe it's not ill-gotten gains,' I said. 'Maybe some well-meaning rich person has hidden some perfectly legitimate treasure, and wants to reward intelligence by seeing who can work out where it is?'

'Maybe,' said Mark, 'and maybe in the same la la cuckoo-land where that's true, Mrs Doris Bud, wife of our beloved leader Captain Bud, is going to be the next big catwalk model, and I do mean big – I mean, they'd have to reinforce the catwalk first – because, Luke, people in the real world just aren't that nice. There aren't any well-meaning rich people who want to give you treasure. Get used to it.'

'I don't know what kind of sad life you've had, Mark,' I said to him, shaking my head, 'but it's not true that nobody out there is nice. There are nice people.'

Mark turned to Matt and said, 'You'd better teach your little boyfriend some cold hard facts of life, pretty boy, because he is such a babe in the woods, he is going to get eaten up.' He said something to Eoin, and the two of them sauntered off.

Star looked between me and Matt and back again, obviously having heard Mark calling me Matt's boyfriend, and asked, 'Are you two . . . ?'

'NO!' we shouted in unison.

'Okay,' she said, holding her hands up to ward off the force of our denial. 'Just asking.'

The awkward silence was broken by Tyler, the one

who had called us 'British dudes' earlier and who had the palest blond hair that I've ever seen. He said, 'You know what, though, I heard this rumour, right, from my buddy who moved to Atlanta, who got it from his cousin who came to Camp Hope like three years ago or something, that the year before he was at camp, three kids disappeared from one of the cabins in the middle of the night and they were never found again. They had the local sheriff in, and like search and rescue teams as well, and maybe even the FBI, but no one could work out who or what took them, and what happened to them. They had to close the camp and send everyone home, but it opened again the next year as usual, and none of the counsellors would talk about it, or even admit that it happened.'

There was silence after his speech, while we took it in.

'What if,' said the girl beside Star, who like Natalie's buddy Ashley was so quiet as to be little more than scenery, 'what if they were lured away with some coded messages? What if the person who lured them is back, and is out to get *us* now?'

We looked at the note now like it was something dangerous. As if the very words and the paper had the power to do us harm.

'Come on!' said Star, her voice shattering the tension that was building around the note. 'Rumour shmumour – I was here last year and no one said anything about mysteriously missing kids. I bet your cousin's next-door neighbour's dog, or whoever it was who told you that story, was just yanking your chain. You know, trying to make you scared to go to camp. What camp doesn't have spooky rumours? I'm surprised they didn't tell you that the souls of the lost kids come back and haunt the cabins and mix up everybody's shoes or something like that.'

'Hey,' said Marco, 'I heard that story. No, seriously I did. The ghosts of the missing kids come into the cabins at night and mix up your shoes, and if you listen very closely . . .' He lowered his voice and whispered the next sentence, making us all lean in and strain to hear him: 'If you listen very closely, in the middle of the night, when everyone else is sleeping, you might hear them go . . . YAAAGH!'

Everyone jumped when Marco yelled, and then we all fell about laughing. Laughing at ourselves for being taken in by his joke, but also laughing because we were relieved that no one seemed to be taking the threat of bad guys seriously any more.

Captain Bud stood up then to tell us it was time to get ready for bed, and to announce that there would be flag-raising in the morning before breakfast, and that we were to congregate at the flag-pole in front of the archery range.

I picked up the now-decoded message and brought it with me, somehow feeling that it was my property, since I was the one who found it.

The message said, 'Follow the clues', so I knew there would be more clues coming. In spite of Tyler's story about missing campers, I didn't think anything bad would come of the clues. I was excited and intrigued, but not worried – not then. It was all still a game to me then.

*

Camp was a lot more crowded after the Americans arrived, and even though we'd only been there a day longer, and it was their country, I still felt a bit territorial, like they were invading our space.

In the morning the shower block was a nightmare, with people everywhere you turned, and then before breakfast there was the first flag-raising.

We wandered over to the archery range in the thin morning sunshine waiting to see what would happen. The counsellors organised us, lining up the Brits on one side and the Americans on the other.

The bugle player was back (it was a busy morning for him) and he played a tune that I recognised as something American, while two girls slow-marched up to the flag-pole holding a neatly folded flag in their outstretched arms. The American line all brought the clenched fists of their right hands up to rest over their hearts, and gazed lovingly at the flag while it was attached to the ropes of the flag-pole and solemnly raised.

Then the bugle stopped, and led by Captain Bud, the campers recited the Pledge of Allegiance:

> I pledge allegiance to the flag,
> Of the United States of America,
> And to the republic, for which it stands,
> One nation, under God, indivisible,
> With liberty and justice for all.

Then the ceremony ended and everyone went for breakfast.

★

After breakfast I went back to my favourite spot by the lake to give myself an insulin shot. I didn't see any lizards, but I saw an absolutely amazing dragonfly. Its body was as big as a cigar, and its wings glittered with iridescence like something magical. I didn't care if Mark Blackwell had seen or even dissected a hundred enormous dragonflies since we got here, that one was mine, and I thought it was awesome.

That day we had kayaking. Yet again, most of the time was spent learning the names of the pieces of equipment, but we did make it into the water eventually. The lake has different areas roped off: one for swimming, one for kayaking, and others for fishing or other water activities. Kneeling in the boats was pretty sore on the knees, plus there was water sloshing around the bottom of the kayaks, so it was pretty damp too. We learned to roll the kayaks, turning the boat through 360 degrees, so that for a couple of seconds you're actually upside down under the water. We had these plastic skirt things that go around your waist and then attach to the boat which are supposed to stop too much water from getting in, but water still did get in, plus your top half is drenched anyway. It was cool, though.

By the time we got out of the water, it was really warm, so it felt good being wet. The lake water was pretty clean, although I did find some slimy bits of plant stuck to the back of my T-shirt. Matt and I didn't bother going back to our cabins to change before hiking, figuring we'd be dry soon enough, and just wandered over to the hiking store and got our bags ready before the rest of the kids turned up. Natalie and Ashley arrived when we had just finished filling up our water canteens.

'Hey,' said Matt to the girls, 'ready to hit the trail?'

Jack and Arash had come up behind the girls, and Jack answered before the girls could: 'I don't know why we have to do this stupid hiking anyway. It's prehistoric. No one needs to walk anywhere any more. Haven't they heard of cars?'

'You can't get so close to nature in a car,' Natalie said.

'If I wanted to get close to nature,' Jack replied, 'I'd watch the Discovery Channel.'

Arleen the hiking instructor arrived then and said, 'You're going to love hiking – I promise. We're doing the bog walk today.'

We looked at each other with raised eyebrows. A bog walk didn't sound like something to be happy about.

'Hurry up, get your bags packed,' Arleen said. 'We need to get a move on, guys.'

We trooped over to the edge of the forest, and Arleen told us to follow the green arrows. As we walked, she pointed out things like flowers or the tracks made by small animals or birds. Sometimes she pointed out things that were edible: 'This fungus has a delicious smoky flavour, but this one is highly poisonous – and this one won't kill you, but it'll induce vomiting.'

After we'd been walking for about ten minutes, Arleen's running commentary slowed down, and I took the opportunity to ask her about the missing campers.

'Missing campers?' she said. 'Where d'ya hear that? That's not true at all. It's nonsense. It never happened.'

She was talking quickly and I exchanged looks with Matt and Natalie. It was obvious to me from the looks they shot back that they found her vehement denial as suspicious as I did.

'There's absolutely no truth in that rumour, I can assure you. Camp Hope is perfectly safe.' She didn't meet my eye as she said it, then she added, 'I came here when I was a child,' as if that was conclusive proof that nothing bad could have happened.

'But . . .' I pressed, 'aren't there lots of places where people could get lost around the camp? Or where people could hide?'

'What? No . . . well, yes, but it didn't happen, okay? Now look, here's an excellent example of a local wild-flower, the alpine marsh violet: its flowers are fragrant and . . .'

She had obviously changed the subject on purpose. She made it clear that she didn't want the missing campers discussed any further by talking without ceasing about everything we passed, from plants to geographical features, for the rest of the hike.

After another ten minutes or so, we left the woods and walked over scrubland, picking our way between the low bushes. When we'd covered a fair bit of ground, Arleen shouted for us all to stop, although I couldn't see why. The only difference I could notice about the way ahead was that it looked a little greener than behind us, the grass grew higher and there were fewer bushes. I also noticed swarms of midges – those annoying little insects that hover in clouds around rivers and get in your mouth – but I didn't realise we'd hit the bog until Arleen told us all to take off our shoes and socks and follow her. She stepped into the grassy field and sank almost up to her knees.

Tentatively, we began to follow her. As one or two people stepped into the grass, they made disgusted noises, and lifted their feet with squelching, sucking sounds. Intrigued, I stepped in, and felt the weirdest series of sensations. First wetness – the grass was growing through water, which wasn't obvious until you were looking down at it – then thick sloppy mud. My feet sank into the cool mud and I could feel its sliminess oozing up between my toes.

A memory from way back flooded into my mind, triggered by the feeling of mud between my toes.

I was about eight or nine. It was in Natalie's garden. Her family were getting a new lawn laid, so men had been in digging up the old turf for days, and new rolls of grass that looked like carpet were stacked up at the side of the house ready to be rolled out and fitted together like patchwork. It was raining, so the workmen had gone inside for a cup of tea. Natalie and I had slipped out unnoticed and taken off our shoes and socks to walk on the dirt that was rapidly turning into mud. Worms had risen to the surface, and we chased off the birds that were hovering hopefully overhead and grabbed the brown, sticky creatures in our still chubby childish hands. I remember the smell of the earth wetted by the new rain. I remember the feel of the worms like jelly-sweets in my fingers, and the mud, cold and slippery under my feet. We were laughing, Natalie and I. She was manic, which was not like her. She was normally a careful, considered child – always neat and organised. I don't think it crossed my little-boy mind to wonder why she was running about barefoot in the mud, I just felt jubilant, excited, seizing the moment without analysing it.

Natalie's dad came out, looking angry. Uh oh, I thought, we're in trouble now. But Natalie ignored him – if anything she became wilder. Her foot slipped from under her and she landed on her bottom, but instead of getting up, she giggled and lay down, making mud-angels with her arms and legs.

'NATALIE!' yelled Mr Anderson, with all the force of an angry dad – something I understood. At that age it would have made me hang my head and wait for the inevitable punishment.

But Natalie stood up with her hands on her hips and her head held high, a picture of muddy defiance, and yelled back:

'I DON'T HAVE TO DO WHAT YOU TELL ME. YOU'RE NOT MY DAD!'

Mr Anderson, who I'd always thought *was* Natalie's dad, looked stunned. He didn't say, 'Don't be ridiculous, Natalie, of course I'm your dad – do as you're told.' He just stared at her, then turned around and went back inside. We watched him go, and then with all the subtlety of a nine-year-old, I threw a worm at Natalie, which she caught triumphantly and threw back.

I watched Natalie now, steadying herself with her hand on Ashley's shoulder. Matt was making his way over to them, and I noticed that several other girls were watching *his* progress.

I thought back to the past again. My mum had screamed at the sight of me, coming home through the back door, covered in mud and holding my shoes in my hands. She'd put me straight in the bath, and I'd asked her about Mr Anderson. 'Why is Natalie's dad not her dad?'

'Oh,' my mum had said, looking worried. 'Well, Natalie's mum was married to a different man when Natalie was born. But they, um, broke up, and then she married Mr Anderson.'

At the time I hadn't thought about it much, but now I wondered what had happened to Natalie's real dad. Why did she go and live with her aunt and uncle after the accident with her mum and stepdad? Why didn't she go and live with her real dad?

- Five -
THE CAMP HOPE MONSTER

That afternoon we had abseiling, which was a big let-down (no pun intended). I'm not afraid of heights at all, and I couldn't wait to launch off the abseiling platform, but they didn't even let us get off the ground in the first lesson. More learning the names of pieces of equipment. My head was swimming with karabiner clips and snaffle bits. Okay, I thought, so it's important to know what you're doing before launching yourself off a cliff, but does it really matter whether or not you know the correct pronunciation of the name of the little bit of metal that's saving your life? I thought the idea of the camp was for us to learn to be less nerdy . . .

In the hour between abseiling and dinner, there was an activity called 'Talk Time'. It was reminiscent of the sessions in Mr Kenyan's office that Natalie and I had missed PE for. One of the counsellors (thankfully not Drew) sat down with a group of us around the burned-out remains of the campfire and tried to get us to talk about various topics. A girl called Jane got quite worked up about climate change, and a couple of boys from the cabin beside ours almost had a fist fight over the best strategy in some video game. Arash kept chirping up with anagrams of everyone's name. I hate having to talk in front of a group so I pretty much kept quiet.

After dinner we hung around in the dining hall again, and then a bunch of us left together with our torches to walk over to the stables and see the horses. Personally, going to the stink zone wasn't my idea of a fun way to spend an evening, but some of the girls wanted to coo over the luverly ponies, so we went along with it. Half-way across the field to the stables Star said, 'Stop, everybody.'

'What? What is it?' several people asked.

'Get ready,' she said. 'On the count of three, everyone turn off your flashlights.'

We did – Star has this quality about her that makes people obey her without question – and the effect was astonishing. It became all of a sudden darker than I imagined it was possible to be. I held my hand in front of my face and literally could see nothing. I tried opening and closing my eyes a few times to see if it made any difference – and it didn't. I could hear the others breathing, and making little gasping noises as they too were blown away by the complete darkness. No streetlights, no electricity, no neon advertisements. We were in the middle of nowhere, on the other side of the earth from the sun, and it was dark.

'Now,' said Star, 'look up and meet my namesakes.'

Whoa. When people described something as being as numerous as the stars in the sky, it never before meant to me what it would do now after that sight. The sky was pebble-dashed with diamonds. At home we have a moth-eaten old curtain. It's dark blue, and thick, but when it's drawn against the sunny window the millions of holes show up as pinpricks of light, and the sky above Camp Hope that night could have been a huge moth-eaten curtain holding back the brilliance of the universe.

I stood and stared, entranced. I could almost feel the world turning beneath me and see the dance of the Milky Way to the music of the comets and gas giants and red dwarfs and whatever other wonders are out there.

'AIEEEEEEEE!'

Someone screamed, breaking through my feelings of awe like a bucket of ice. In the confusion that followed I almost fell over backwards, and fumbled my torch, dropping it at my feet. Other people turned on their torches, and in the haloes of light I was able to retrieve mine, and add it to the blinding beams everyone was pointing in everyone else's face.

'What the . . . ?'

'Who . . . ?

'What . . . ?'

'Something grabbed me!' Star's friend Shelly said, looking around wildly. 'It was dark, and I was looking at the stars, and all of a sudden something grabbed me!'

We pointed the torches around us to see if we could reveal who or what had grabbed Shelly. The beams of light fell on tree trunks and the fencing around the horses' corral. There was no sign of movement and no noise apart from our own loud breathing and the distant sound of other campers chatting and laughing.

Suddenly the darkness seemed less awesome and more ominous. The tiny circle of light on the ground in front of me seemed woefully inadequate, and I was tempted to spin around to let the torchlight chase away unimaginable things that might be creeping up behind me. All of us moved closer together. Star was beside me, and I could feel the warmth of her arm next to mine and smell the clean fruity smell that came off her hair. She grabbed my hand and I felt a thrill that was nothing to do with fear course up my body.

Matt put his arms around Natalie and her friend Ashley, and said, in a mock–manly voice, 'Don't worry, girls, I'll protect you from the Camp Hope Monster.' Natalie looked like she wanted to wriggle out of his grasp, but then her eyes travelled down my arm to mine and Star's linked hands and instead she said, 'Would you walk us back to our cabin, Matt? Not that I'm scared or anything, just – y'know.'

Just then a horse made a loud, unexpected whinnying sound and most of us, including Natalie, jumped and screamed.

'Okay,' Natalie said, laughing, 'so I am scared.'

'Never fear, ladies,' Matt said. 'Matt is here.' He leaned over to me and said quietly, 'You'll come too, Luke – all right, mate?'

Matt and I walked with the girls over to their cabins while the other boys went back to ours.

By the time Matt and I got back, Zach and KC were holding up a white piece of paper and one of them was saying, 'Check this out, you guys — another mystery clue.'

I wondered briefly if the same person who had grabbed Shelly by the horse corral had left the clue in our cabin.

Zach held his torch over the note and I saw that what was written on it was a series of numbers:

20·8·9·19 − 3·12·21·5 − 9·19 − 16·18·5·20·20·25 − 5·1·19·25, − 2·21·20 −

4·15·14·20 − 7·5·20 − 20·15·15 − 12·1·26·25.

6·15·18 − 14·5·24·20 − 20·9·13·5 − 25·15·21·12·12 − 14·5·5·4 − 20·15 −

11·14·15·23 − 23·8·1·20 − 3·12·25·20·9·5 − 2·5·3·1·13·5 − (20·8·5 − 2·9·7·7·5·19·20 −

4·1·9·19·25).

It was too late to try and work out the coded message by then, and too dark in the torchlight. I was hoping (and it turned out that I was right) that it was just a simple number substitution anyway: A=1, B=2, etc. When Drew came into the cabin and told us to be quiet I put away the clue in the pocket of my shorts to look at the next day.

In the morning Drew told us we were going to have a sleep-out in the woods on Saturday night, just us Chipmunks. We had to build a shelter, and then sleep in it, and we also had to cook our dinner and breakfast on fires we'd built ourselves. Some of the boys looked quite excited by the news, but my heart sank. For one thing, being alone in the woods with Drew and whatever else was out there didn't seem like such a good idea. Okay, in the cold light of morning I didn't feel as spooked as I had the night before, but that didn't mean I wanted to take stupid risks. And even if there wasn't anything to be afraid of — if the missing campers rumours were not true and Shelly had imagined being grabbed — I still didn't fancy camping out. Our woodcraft skills were really not that good. Matt and I had not yet managed to build a successful fire, and as for building our own shelter — it was just comical. I could see us running around like a speeded-up film with silly music playing, bumping into each other and knocking everything over. Like the Chuckle Brothers times ten. I thought it was going to be a disaster.

We had fire-building that morning, and just to prove me right, our fire once again failed to light. Then we had our first fencing lesson. I wondered if I would be able to defend myself against a real attack with a fencing foil. Probably not, since the swords were blunt and bendy. It might hurt a bit if I twanged it at somebody.

In the afternoon we had swimming, and for once the instructor just told us to jump in and have fun. Matt and I decided to use the time to ask some of the other kids if they'd had any mysterious clues appearing in their cabins. We went about amongst different groups of kids who were splashing around and tried to get them to give us their attention for a moment. Some of them took us seriously, and some of them just thought we were coming over for a splash war. Nobody admitted to having found any clues, though, which was a little bit confusing. If the treasure hunt was being set up by the camp, which I still thought was probably the case, then why was our cabin the only one to receive any clues? It didn't really add up.

We gave up trying to have sensible conversations after a while and just started to have some fun. It was hot and the water felt good – and swimming in a lake was much cooler than swimming in the public baths at home.

After we'd been in the water for about an hour, the sky suddenly darkened with clouds and fat drops of rain started to add ripples to the already turbulent water.

The storm was as ferocious as it was sudden, and pretty quickly the instructor blew two sharp blasts on his whistle, which was the signal for everyone to get out. He did a quick head-count as we stood dripping and wrapped in towels, then sent us into the changing rooms to get into dry clothes.

It was kind of futile putting on dry things since the rain was so heavy by the time we were ready to leave that we were instantly soaked again. The air was still warm, and the rain was coming down so fast that it actually hurt. The sky was really dark by then, and I felt the hairs on my arms tingle as if the air was filled with electricity. I guess it was, because moments later the sky was split in two by the coolest bolt of forked lightning I had ever seen. The blast of the thunder coincided almost exactly with the flash of the lightning, meaning the storm was pretty much right on top of us. We ran to the main hall, where most of the other campers were already congregated, standing dripping in front of the fire, or else crowded around the windows watching the spectacular light show. The air was steamy with evaporating wetness, and I saw a few people with glasses repeatedly having to take them off to wipe the condensation clear. I looked around for familiar faces, and saw Natalie and Ashley over by the fire. I pointed them out to Matt, and we went over to them.

'Hey!' said Natalie, smiling up at us. 'What about this storm – did you ever see such brilliant lightning?'

'I don't like it,' said Ashley, flinching as fresh thunder rolled.

'Don't worry,' said Matt. 'People hardly ever get hit by lightning.'

Ashley didn't look very comforted.

'Oh, guess what?' I said, suddenly remembering the new coded message that I hadn't looked at since Zach handed it over to me the night before. 'Another clue.'

I took the crumpled note from the pocket of my shorts. The edges where it was folded had got wet from the rain, and the paper almost tore as I unfolded it to show the girls.

Natalie held it gingerly, and it flapped in the hot waves of air coming off the fire. 'We should go over to a table and look at it properly,' she said.

Some other people joined us as we went over to a table. News of the first coded message had spread around the camp, and lots of people wanted to see the new one. Fresh paper and pencils were found from somewhere, and the note was spread out in the middle of the table where everyone could see.

'The numbers are all between one and twenty-six,' someone said. 'They're probably just the position of letters in the alphabet.'

'Yeah,' said somebody else, 'that would make the first word, um . . .' He started counting on his fingers, and I noticed that lots of people were tapping their own fingers as if they were counting too.

'T . . . H . . . I . . . S – this!'

I looked at the faces around the table, and then around the room.

'Where's Star?' I said, realising that I couldn't see her anywhere.

Natalie looked up from the paper on which she was writing the word 'this' under the first group of numbers, and I thought she had an angry expression on her face.

I stood up, and said I was going to go look for her.

'But Luke,' said Natalie, sounding exasperated, 'what about the clue?'

'Look, it's dark outside,' I said, pointing to the windows that were being lashed with rain, 'and everyone else is in here – what if she's in trouble? What if she's hurt? What if –' I left the last sentence hanging, not really knowing what it was that I was afraid of.

'I'll be back soon,' I said, shrugging. 'Carry on without me.'

I went over to the door and braced myself for going outside in the rain. Before I opened the door, though, I peered through the window beside it, cupping my hands around my eyes so I could see out into the gloom.

There were two figures out there, one tugging at the other. Were they fighting? Was someone attacking Star? I was just about to run out of the door when I realised that they were not fighting. One of the figures *was* Star. She was standing with her face raised and her arms outstretched as if she was embracing the storm. She was slowly rotating on the spot – her back had been to me at first, but when she turned I saw her face and knew it was her. Her feet were slipping slightly as her trainers lost their grip on the wet earth. I wondered if Star had lost her grip on reality – standing out in the rain like that. And yet she looked so happy, so alive, that I almost wanted to go out there and get soaked with her. The other, smaller person was Star's friend Shelly. She was tugging at Star's arm trying to get her to come in. Finally Shelly got her attention, and Star lowered her arms and followed her over to the door beside the window where I stood.

They came in, dripping water, and Star saw me by the door and smiled.

'I was worried about you,' I said, stupidly.

She started to say something, but before she could, the camp counsellors arrived from wherever they had been hiding out from the storm, coming through the door from the kitchen, and announced that it was time to get the tables ready for dinner.

It seemed later than dinnertime, because it was so dark, but when savoury smells started wafting in from the kitchen, I realised that my body was ready to eat. Dinner was macaroni and cheese, with some kind of horrible salady stuff on the side. When it was eaten and cleared up, and after I'd gone off to the loo to sort out my insulin, the code breakers re-formed, joined by Star and Shelly. Natalie took the now almost finished translation out of her pocket and laid it on the table:

20.8.9.19 – 3.12.21.5 – 9.19 – 16.18.5.20.20.25 – 5.1.19.25, – 2.21.20 –
T H I S   C L U E   I S   P R E T T Y   E A S Y,   B U T

4.15.14.20 – 7.5.20 – 20.15.15 – 12.1.26.25.
D O N 'T   G E T   T O O   L A Z Y.

6.15.18 – 14.5.24.20 – 20.9.13.5 – 25.15.21.'12.12 – 14.5.5.4 – 20.15 –
F O R   N E X T   T I M E   Y O U'L L   N E E D   T O

11.14.15.23 – 23.8.1.20 – 3.12.25.20.9.5 – 2.5.3.1.13.5 – (20.8.5 – 2.9.7.7.5.19.20 –
K N O W   W H A T   C L Y T I E   B E C A M E   (T H E   B I G G E S T

4.1.9.19.25).
D A I S Y).

We quickly worked out what the last three words were: 'the biggest daisy' – not that they made much sense.

THIS CLUE IS PRETTY EASY, BUT
DON'T GET TOO LAZY.
FOR NEXT TIME YOU'LL NEED TO KNOW WHAT
CLYTIE BECAME (THE BIGGEST
DAISY).

Once again the clue caused more confusion after it was decoded than before. Who or what was Clytie? What did it become? And what's the deal with daisies?

I was completely stumped, but around the table conversation was buzzing. Arash was muttering something about daisies being from the family Asteraceae, and whether something was strictly speaking the biggest family member when its flower heads were not single flowers but rather clusters of ray florets and disc florets; nevertheless, he would have to say that the clue was probably referring to the –

At the same time, Star was saying that in Greek mythology, Clytie fell in love with the god Apollo, so much so that she couldn't move and had to stand and watch his chariot move across the sky, and that after nine days she turned into a –

'– sunflower.'

They both said the word together, each following it by trying to give at the same time an explanation of how they'd come to that conclusion, so it was several minutes before anyone could hear what they were saying and work out what was going on.

'I reckon,' I said, 'that the next clue must need a keyword to decipher it, and the keyword must be "sunflower".'

'Oh, d'you think?' said Matt sarcastically, and I looked at him, wondering what his problem was.

'Well, obviously, Luke,' said Natalie, and I started to feel a little bit confused about why my two so-called best friends were ganging up against me.

'Cool,' said Star, smiling at me and making me forget about being ticked off. 'How does that work then?'

So I explained to her about keyword ciphers:

'You write down the keyword, in this case SUN-FLOWER, and count how many letters there are in the word. Then you write out the secret message in rows of that number of letters – in this case, nine.' I took the pen and paper from Natalie, and showed Star what I meant. 'Say I wanted to send you a message that said, "Meet me at the lake tomorrow",' I said, 'I would write it like this, under the keyword:

S	U	N	F	L	O	W	E	R
M	E	E	T	M	E	A	T	T
H	E	L	A	K	E	T	O	M
O	R	R	O	W	X	Z	X	Y

'You just fill in the blank spaces at the end with random letters.'

'So, what are the spaces at the top for?' Star asked.

'Aha,' I said, 'this is where it gets tricky. You number the letters in the keyword alphabetically. Like this:

7	8	4	2	3	5	9	1	6
S	U	N	F	L	O	W	E	R
M	E	E	T	M	E	A	T	T
H	E	L	A	K	E	T	O	M
O	R	R	O	W	X	Z	X	Y

'Oh!' said Star. 'You draw little lines through your sevens as well? I thought I was the only person in the world who did that.'

I smiled at her, and ignored the gagging noises Matt was making.

'Then you write the letters down in the order of the columns, without writing the letters from the keyword. So, first I'd write column one, which would be TOX, then column two – TAO – then three – MKW – and so on, to get:

TO XTAOM KWE LREEX TM YMHO EER ATZ

'The spaces are random, you just ignore them. The person who has the keyword just has to look at the alphabetical order to know which way to rearrange the message "Meet me at the lake tomorrow".'

'Okay,' said Star, 'I will. What time?'

I stared at her, not understanding at first what she meant. For once, though, I did get my idiot brain to think of something sensible to say in time, and with the corners of my mouth rising without me even telling them to, I said, 'After the fireworks.'

I had just made a date with Star, without even meaning to. I had just made up the 'meet me at the lake' message off the top of my head to illustrate how to do the code. I never thought she would take it as an invitation. But she did. I felt giddy.

A date.

With Star.

Woohoo!

- six -
FIREWORKS

The next day was the Fourth of July – American Independence Day. They had flag-raising, even though it was a Friday and they normally had flag-raising only on Wednesdays. I was wished 'Happy Fourth of July' about a hundred times, by campers and counsellors alike. There was a festive mood in the camp, and a vanload of fireworks had been spotted driving up the lane the previous afternoon, so everyone was looking forward to the display. The weather was much fresher after the storm, and the sky was clear and still – perfect firework weather. Us British kids were a bit bemused by it all: I couldn't really imagine anyone at home getting this excited over the British equivalent to Independence Day, if we had one – I guess we're just not such a patriotic people.

Drew took us Chipmunks on a learning-how-to-make-your-own-shelter session. It was actually not quite as bad as I'd thought. The shelter we had to build was a sort of giant lean-to made out of big branches tied together using these long, stringy grassy plants. We had to weave bushy spruce branches through the framework to give it some insulation. We got about half-way through building it in the time we had, and Drew said we could finish it off when we went out the next night. He said that when it was finished it would be shaped like a big wedge, and we'd all scoot inside in our sleeping bags with our feet in the narrow end and our heads in the open end. Drew had said something at the beginning about aligning it in the right direction so that the wind would blow over it in the night, and not into the opening, but I'm not sure that anyone really paid attention to him, and the way he smirked at us while we were building looked worryingly like he was happy to see us making trouble for ourselves.

In the afternoon I got to learn how to hold a sword in fencing (big whoop), and then we had nature studies, which is the most boring thing ever. We sat in this sort of barn thing looking at pictures of leaves.

All day long, though, my mind was preoccupied with my date with Star. Was it a date? Would I act like a complete idiot and muck up my chances of ever getting anywhere with a girl ever?

When Brandy, the nature instructor, was droning on about leaf shapes, I was trying to think up smooth things I could say to Star. Like that all the millions of stars we saw in the sky the other night paled in comparison to her face, or that she was everything I could ever have dreamed of in a girl if I was the best, most imaginative dreamer ever.

I know. Lame, naff, stupid.

At dinnertime I couldn't even bring myself to look at Star. At least, not unless I happened to notice that she was looking in the other direction, and then I gazed at the back of her head like it was some kind of work of art, entranced by the way her hair fell down her back in ripples like flowing lava . . .

Anyway.

After dinner we all went out and stood in front of the cabin to watch the fireworks. They were pretty cool. Not as good as some of the big displays I've been to on Bonfire Night, but better than the economy box of sad spluttering candles my dad usually buys for our back garden. After the fireworks, steaming mugs of cocoa were brought out on trays and passed around. I refused the mug that was offered to me. It would have been nice to have a warm drink, a cup of tea or something, but I didn't need any more sugar after my dinner. Matt was cradling his mug when he sidled up to me and said, 'So, when are you going to the lake then?'

Of course Matt knew. Everybody knew. We'd been in the middle of a crowded table of people when Star and I had organised our little tryst, even if it had seemed like we were the only people there. In fact, lots of people were looking over at me and Matt curiously, as if my date with Star had been laid on for their personal entertainment. I looked over at the girls, to see if they were also watching the spectacle, and realised that Star was not amongst them.

'Oh, later,' I told Matt. 'I'm going to the loo.' I waved my injector pen at him to imply that I needed a shot, and he shrugged and went to talk to some other boys.

I went into the loo, but once I was inside, I turned off my torch and came straight out again, feeling my way in the darkness until I was out of sight of the others.

Star was standing by the lake like something out of an Arthurian fantasy. I instinctively looked over at the water, expecting to see a sword hilt rising from the middle of the lake. But it wasn't a fantasy, and there was no sword.

'Well met, fine sir,' she said, in a passable attempt at an English accent.

My heart thudded in my chest and for some reason just managing to stay standing seemed to be taking up all my concentration. 'Star' was all I could say, my voice giving an embarrassing squeak, reminding me that it wasn't that long ago that I sounded like a soprano choir-boy.

She smiled and held out her hands, and without me having to say anything else, she pulled me close to her, and we kissed.

I could still see the fireworks when I closed my eyes.

In the morning, when I was doing my after-breakfast blood test, sitting in the very spot where I'd met up with Star, it felt more like a dream than something that had really happened. I could still see her in my mind looking weirdly silvery in the moonlight, and dream or no dream, just the thought of her did funny things to my body.

The schedule for the day was different because it was a Saturday, and at least half of the Saturdays at Camp

Hope are given over to 'team-building' and other 'self-affirming' activities. All over the place people were being forced to hug each other, or catch their falling cabin mates, or worse still, share their innermost fears and insecurities with 'the group'.

When we were told to go and introduce ourselves to someone we'd never spoken to before, instead I looked around for a familiar face. Matt was shifting backwards and forwards on his feet looking like he wanted to escape from a short, freckled American boy wearing glasses and talking animatedly about the differences between British and American plant life. I decided (somewhat wickedly) to leave him to it, and looked around some more. Star was waving her arms while talking to a bemused-looking British girl, so I left them alone as well. I saw that Natalie had just finished a conversation with someone so I quickly went over to her.

'Hi,' I said. 'What do you make of all this touchy-feely stuff?'

'The trick is to make up some embarrassing personal fact to tell everyone and then they'll leave you alone,' she said. 'Like "I've got incontinence problems."'

'You didn't?' I said.

'No, not really.' She laughed. 'You think this is embarrassing, though – at least you don't have to sit through Mrs Bud's hygiene talks.'

'What, does she tell you how to wash or something?'

'Pretty much, yeah. I think Americans think they're the only clean people in the world,' Natalie said. 'Last night she explained to all the British girls how to use a razor to shave our legs and armpits – like we didn't know!

'She's creepy, though,' she went on. 'She comes into our cabins and asks us how we're feeling and if we want to talk about anything. We've all started pretending we're asleep, or else that we're rushing off to something whenever she comes.

'Talking of creepy, what about your counsellor, Drew? I wouldn't go and sleep out in the woods with him!'

'Thanks for reminding me,' I said. 'Do you see how he plays with that knife all the time? Like he's dying to use it on someone?' Images of a knife massacre in the woods flashed through my mind. 'At least there'll be ten of us against only one of him – we could fight him off.'

'Yeah, unless he drugs you,' Natalie said. She wasn't being very comforting.

We stood in silence for a couple of minutes, and then Natalie said, 'Do you think it's Drew who's sending the messages?'

'I don't know,' I said. 'It could be, but somehow it doesn't seem like his style. I mean, if the treasure hunt is supposed to lure us away from the camp so someone can abduct us, if it was Drew then he could just get us on the sleep-out – so why would he bother with all the code-breaking stuff?'

'Yeah, I guess you've got a point.' Natalie said. 'Who do you think it is then?'

'I don't know – I still think the clues are innocent. I

think they're set up by the camp as a test or a competition or something. Don't you?'

'Yeah,' said Natalie. 'Maybe.'

Someone blew a whistle just then to announce the end of the session.

Lunch was an open-air barbecue presided over by Captain Bud wearing a chef's hat and flipping burgers and hot dogs like it was an art form, and the afternoon was free time. Matt and I decided to go swimming, and when we were getting our trunks from the cabin, Matt asked me, 'So, how far d'you get with Star then? Did you break the twenty-centimetre rule?'

It was one of the official camp rules that girls and boys were not allowed within twenty centimetres of each other. I pretended not to hear him, so he pressed on: 'Come on, you can tell me.'

I thought about how to put into words what had happened between me and Star.

'Well . . .' I began.

Matt didn't wait for me to go on, though. He was obviously bursting to tell me something himself, and cut across me.

'I'll tell you about my date with Natalie.'

'What!'

The warm fuzzy feeling I got when I thought about Star evaporated when his words filtered through. Matt had had a date with Natalie? But Natalie was *my* friend – *my* old Mr Kenyan's class buddy. What was Matt doing going out with her? What was she doing going out with Matt?

'What date?' I said, and my words sounded con-
frontational.

'Hey, chill out, buddy,' Matt said, holding up his
hands. 'You can't keep all the girls to yourself. Natalie
finds me fascinating.'

I wanted to tell him to leave her alone, to go off with
one of the muffin-top girls, or any of the countless
other girls that had been giving him moon eyes all over
the place. But I didn't. I just said, 'Whatever. Are we
going swimming, or what?'

I don't know why it annoyed me so much that Matt
was going out with Natalie. It's not like I fancied her or
anything.

At five o'clock we had to meet up with the other guys
from the cabin and go with Drew into the woods. The
way he smiled and rubbed his hands together didn't help
my feelings of unease as we followed him down the trail.
There was always something dangerous about Drew. He
never actually hit anyone or anything like that, but there
was an undercurrent of threat about him from the beginning that made us obey him without question. It turned
out that Drew's rules, the ones he'd mentioned on the
first night, were pretty much things that he made up as he
went along. Like, kids weren't supposed to be allowed out
of the cabins at night unless the counsellor went with
them, but if anyone asked if they could go to the loo,
Drew would say something like 'Rule number twenty-
seven: Drew does not get out of bed for nobody, so you
just have to hold it in, *comprende*?'

Basically, all Drew's rules were designed to make his

life easier and to stop us annoying him. Even Mark would back down in a challenge against Drew's authority, which I guess is pretty good, because who knows what he'd have got up to if we'd had a nice smiley counsellor.

So anyway, we all met up at the edge of the woods where some firewood logs and cooking pots had been stacked in readiness. Drew told us to bring the stuff, as well as our sleeping bags, and follow him. No one dared complain that he didn't seem to be carrying anything. The lean-to that we had begun to build the day before was in a clearing in the woods about fifteen minutes' walk from the cabins. It was a long enough walk carrying our sleeping bags, and the two fat logs that I'd lifted were a lot heavier than they looked. By the time we got there, I was sweating and my fingers hurt where the edges of the chopped firewood had dug into them.

There was evidence of previous sleep-outs in the charred circles on the ground at the campsite, and Drew told some of us to clear one of them so we could get our new fire started. He explained how to build what he called a 'hunter's fire' by placing two fat logs in a V shape, and filling the cavity between them with kindling and laying sticks of timber across the top. 'We need to keep feeding that fire until the logs get good and red, then we can sit our cooking pot on top and cook us up some stew,' he said.

Once the fire was lit, Drew told us to go and fetch water from a stream that wasn't too far away at least, and when we got back there were potatoes to wash and wrap in foil and bury in the ash that had already started to form at the base of the fire. It was not dark yet, and I was almost beginning to enjoy the boy-scout feel of the open-air cooking – until we found out what was going to be the main course.

Drew said, 'Now, boys, I could have got us a nice big can of stew from the camp kitchens for us to cook up, but that ain't real living rough, is it? So with that in mind, I may have taken a stroll earlier and set up some coney traps, which may not be strictly within camp rules, but who's telling, hey?'

I wasn't quite sure what a coney was, but something about trapping animals in the woods, especially since it was against the rules, made me shudder with guilty excitement. A pot of water was left sitting on the fire, with Zach and KC staying behind to mind it, and we started off after Drew into the woods.

He was ahead of us, following some sort of trail he'd left and so when he stopped and swore loudly, we didn't at first see what the problem was. When we caught him up, and crowded around him, following his gaze to the ground, my first instinct was to gag.

Obviously, one of his traps had been successful, but the rabbit that had been caught was, shall we say, no longer intact.

Drew swore loudly and spat on the ground. 'Must have been a coyote, stolen our supper,' he growled. 'We'd best hope the other traps have been left alone or we are going to be hungry.' He stomped off along the trail, but I couldn't help staying and staring at the remains of the rabbit. Its head was undamaged, with the wire of the trap tight around its neck. Beyond the neck, though, not much remained, and what was there was making my stomach lurch uncomfortably, and a sour taste rise to my mouth. The coyote, or whatever it was that had raided the trap, had literally torn the unfortunate rabbit apart. Stupidly I felt tears sting my eyes. I don't know if I was feeling sorry for the rabbit, or if it was just the horror of the scene, but either way I hastily wiped the tears away before anyone saw them, and hurried after the others.

By the time I caught up, Drew was triumphantly holding a second rabbit in the air by its feet. It was struggling weakly in the last throes of life, and watching Drew casually twist its neck to finish it off disturbed me almost as much as seeing the torn carcass moments before. A second rabbit was found and killed, and then we brought our booty back to camp.

Drew delighted in showing us how to skin and gut the conies, as he called them, using his evil-looking knife which he slipped back into his pocket after wiping off the blood when he'd finished. Then he gave us tasks chopping onions and carrots and herbs, and they were all thrown in the pot with some salt and the now chopped-up rabbits. In spite of the bloodiness of its beginnings, the stew quickly started to smell delicious and make my mouth water.

While the stew was cooking, we worked on finishing the lean-to shelter, and laying out our sleeping bags.

Drew had a one-man tent which he pitched along the open end of the lean-to – none of us would dare to complain that that wasn't fair. He also had one of those roll-up camping mattresses and some other stuff that he must have left down earlier. He watched, amused, while we finished our shelter-building. True to form, Marco made jokes and Mark made snide comments while most of us just complained about having to do manual labour. Arash was going on about some 'perfect angle' that keeps coming up in nature, as well as some other thing called the 'perfect ratio', and how nature is like this big beautiful mathematical equation and can be represented as some kind of colourful repeating spiral pattern or something like that. Man, I thought I was clever, but Arash seemed to be on a whole different level of smartness.

Finally we got to sit down and eat. I was hungry, in spite of my feelings of nervousness about being out in the woods, and the food was hot and delicious. When we'd finished, all the leftovers had to be sealed into plastic bags, to stop wild animals from smelling them and coming to investigate in the night. When Drew told us that, I had a sudden urge to pee, and excused myself to go behind a tree, and then wished I hadn't because I was imagining all kinds of wild animals smelling me peeing and wanting to investigate me.

We had to take the enamel dishes from which we'd eaten our dinner down to the stream, and wash them. As we left the glow of the fire we realised how dark it had become. We made pools of light with our torches on the ground in front of our feet, so we could pick out a path to take without tripping. Once again, I had to keep suppressing the urge to spin around with my torch and check there was nothing behind me. Noises spooked us: hooting, breathing, twigs snapping. I was convinced I could see movement in my peripheral vision, even though it was too dark to see anything.

On the way back a voice came out of the darkness with a familiar Southern drawl: 'I've got you now, boys.'

'AAAHHH!' I screamed, along with at least two other boys, and we raised our torches to see Matt laughing back at us. 'Did youse young 'uns all think I was Drew?' he said.

I swore at Matt, and called him an idiot. 'Well, that's not very nice,' he said, still keeping up the Southern accent.

When we got back, Drew was feeding the fire while dragging idly on a cigarette.

I did my insulin shot in front of the others, which I hate doing, but I was starting to get paranoid about being out of sight of the campfire.

Mark asked Drew for a cigarette, and Drew said, 'Now we all know that cigarettes are banned at Camp Hope, on account of them being hazardous to your health, and hazardous to your safety, so why would I have such a thing?'

The fact that he was plainly smoking in front of us hung in the air, and as Mark began to splutter his objections, Drew blew a smoky cloud in his face, and said, 'There – a freebie.'

We sat around the fire, watching it crackle, and huddling against the approaching night chill. Perhaps hoping that the cigarette had mellowed him, Marco broke Drew's rule number three and asked him a question.

'Say, Drew ... ?'

'What is it?' He didn't sound annoyed, so Marco ploughed on.

'There's this rumour, right, that, um, Tyler's aunt's neighbours ...'

'It was my buddy who moved to Atlanta, who got it from his cousin,' Tyler corrected him.

'Oh right, yeah. Anyway, Tyler's buddy from Atlanta heard from his cousin who was at Camp Hope, that these kids disappeared from their cabin in the middle of the night and were never seen again, and we were, um, just wondering if you knew if that was true.'

Drew pulled on his cigarette and stared into the fire. The air around him seemed to get darker all of a sudden so his face was lit with an eerie flickering orange glow as he contemplated what to say.

I wondered if it was going to be like one of those scenes from a movie where the bad guy confesses everything just before he kills his victims.

seven

CAMP FEAR

'Well now . . .' Drew's voice was soft when he began to speak, and we had to strain to hear him over the noise of the burning branches. 'Officially . . . ' – he pronounced the word with a strong 'oh' at the beginning – 'officially, that never happened. Our good Captain Bud, like many men in authority, believes in his own kind of truth. Whether it's to shelter young minds from the harsher realities of the world, or just to ensure the smooth running of his institution – well, who's to say? But anyway, *he* says it never happened, and we've been told that if anyone asks that's the line we take. Nothing happened, period.

'But . . . I say there's no smoke without fire, and I think it's a little strange that apart from Captain Bud and Doris, none of the staff who were here the year that those three kids were rumoured to have disappeared have been hired again. Almost as if he was trying to hush it up, don't you think?

'Some might say he was wrong to keep the camp going, that the place should have been shut down an' all.

I mean, nobody knows what happened, or whether it will happen again.'

He stopped speaking and there was silence for a while. A twig in the fire snapped loudly, making us all jump and breaking the spell of his words.

'What do you think happened?' KC asked.

'What do I think?' Drew drawled out the words, as if he was amazed at his opinion being asked. 'Well, I think those three kids did disappear. As to what happened to them, well now, it could have been any number of things: maybe those kids decided to go out for a midnight stroll, and fell down a cliff or something – but then why were the bodies never found?'

'Coyotes.' It was Mark who said it, and he sounded almost like he was relishing the thought. 'Maybe they fell and were hurt or unconscious, and coyotes came and tore them up and ate them.'

The thought of the rabbit in the trap was still too fresh in my mind to let my imagination go down that path. I tried to blank it out.

'Coyotes almost never attack people,' Drew said. I didn't like the fact that he said 'almost'. 'They might occasionally, or bears even, but it's not likely.'

'Well, what then?' I said, if only to chase away the image of kids being set upon by beasts. 'What else might have happened to them?'

'Murder,' Drew said, savouring the gasp of fear that his pronouncement provoked.

Murder? Why murder? I thought – why would Drew say that?

84

'Maybe they just ran away,' Marco said. 'They didn't have to be murdered.'

'Or they could have been kidnapped,' said Jack.

'No,' said Arash, 'if they were kidnapped there would have been a ransom note, they would have been returned.'

'There might have been a ransom note,' Matt said. 'Since nobody is telling us anything, we're just guessing. Maybe there was a ransom note, and they were returned and nobody was murdered.'

'Maybe,' said Drew, throwing the stub of his cigarette into the fire. 'The truth is that nobody knows. At least, nobody knows who's telling us anything. Maybe Captain Bud chopped them up and cooked them on the barbecue – he does love his barbecuing.

'Now, boys,' Drew said, 'time to turn in.'

Perfect – I was *so* ready to curl up and go to sleep outside with nothing but branches tied together with bits of plant between me and mad axe murderers or cannibals or carnivorous animals. The others must have been spooked too, because as we all got ready for bed, people kept jumping and yelling if anyone else bumped into them. Arash informed us in whispers that Counsellor Drew is an anagram of 'lower scoundrel', and Jack said Camp Hope should be called Camp No Hope.

'Yeah,' said KC, 'or Camp Fear.'

Camp Fear was right – fear slithered over me like a giant cold slug as I lay down in my sleeping bag. It was pretty cramped inside the lean-to. I had Matt on one side of me and Evil Mark on the other, and if I tried to move, or either one of them tried to move, we ended up banging into each other. Not the most comfortable of situations. Drew put out the fire, and disappeared into his tent. We could see the orange glow of another lit cigarette through the canvas, and the silhouette of his face as he sat up smoking it.

I imagined him falling asleep smoking, and dropping the lit cigarette, setting fire to his tent, which would make our lean-to catch alight, and we wouldn't be able to run away because our sleeping bags would melt in the heat . . . I know, an over-active imagination is a curse.

It was a long night. People say that, and you don't realise just how true it can be. Night-time is usually over in a flash, because you sleep through it, but believe me – that night went on and on for ever, what with feeling claustrophobic, and being generally uncomfortable, and the snoring of the other boys (how could they sleep?), and my mind bringing up images that I really didn't want to see – the bodies of the mysterious missing campers lying broken at the bottom of a cliff and being set upon by coyotes, or worse, by Captain Bud with a meat cleaver. When I finally did go to sleep, I was woken up at who knows what hour of the night by a distant howling. I strained to hear the sound better – to see if I could guess what direction it was coming from, or if it was getting any closer. I started to hear other noises too: a rhythmical tapping, soft rustling, the creaking of trees bending in the night breezes. The noises could be innocent – but what if they're not, I thought. What if someone is leaning against a tree to make it creak, what if the tapping is the sound of someone drumming their fingers, biding their time before taking one of us?

The shape of Drew's body silhouetted by the moonlight hitting his tent shifted, and I heard him grunt in his sleep. I found the sound strangely comforting. If Drew was dangerous then I was glad he was sleeping, and if he was not dangerous, then I was glad he was nearby to protect us from whatever it was. I must have finally gone to sleep because the next thing I knew was Drew telling us to get up.

Man, I was never so happy to hear those words and to see the light of morning.

It was pretty early, but no one wanted to lie in. We had to dismantle the lean-to and get another fire going to cook breakfast, which thankfully hadn't been caught in traps, but was just a packet of porridge that Drew produced from his bag. Then the dishes had to be washed again – washing the porridge pot in a cold stream was not a heap of fun – and everything packed away so the woods were left as we found them.

Trekking back to camp was like returning to civilisation. Even our wooden cabin and the cramped shower block seemed like five-star accommodation after sleeping out in the woods. I almost wanted to bow down and kiss the ground in our cabin, that's how glad I was to be back. I guess I've never really been the adventuresome type.

We were given an hour on Sunday morning to sit somewhere and meditate and find our inner peace, or something wacky like that. Those of us who had been

on the sleep-out were supposed to write down our feelings about that in a notebook. I just spent the hour
writing about building the lean-to, and about Drew's
tale of the missing campers. I felt stiff and sore as I wrote
sitting on my tree-stump by the lake – the ground had
been *very* hard and lumpy.

It did occur to me that if Captain Bud had been
responsible for the kids' disappearance, then it might not
be such a good idea to write about it in a notebook that
he would most probably read, but I dismissed my worries and just wrote it anyway. For all my high IQ I guess
sometimes I'm not that smart.

That afternoon we had to write letters home to our
families, and I realised that I had barely given them a
thought before that. I did kind of miss them when I was
writing the letter – well, not Ryan obviously, but my
mum and dad. Not much, but kind of. Of course it
never crossed my mind as I wrote about fencing and
kayaking and all the other stuff at camp, that my parents
might never see me again. I don't think I even mentioned the clues. Why would I? As far as I knew then,
they were probably just a bit of fun.

After the letters were handed in there was this big camp
pony trek. They had to borrow horses from another camp
to have enough for everyone, and we all got assigned
which ones to ride. Because I'm tall they gave me this
enormous beast of a horse that looked at me through its
beady horse eyes and snorted down its nose at me as if to
say, 'You're horse food, mate.' Star got a big horse too, but
at least hers was graceful looking, not just mean like mine.

Matt's horse was over by Natalie's and I tried to ignore them laughing together as the counsellors helped them to get on. I felt kind of awkward with Star. I've never been particularly eloquent with her and I hadn't spoken to her at all since the night at the lake. Were we boyfriend and girlfriend now? How was I supposed to act? Star looked like she was comfortable around horses so I asked her if she'd ridden before.

'Oh yeah,' she said, 'I dated this guy with his own pony back in junior high – and before that I took riding lessons at my cousin's riding school, so I'm pretty much at home around horses.'

My mind was still stuck on the first thing she said: she dated this guy . . . She said it so casually, as if dating was normal for her and she had tons of experience. Oh crud, I thought. The closest I've got to dating was talking to girls from school, and that had never really led anywhere. Plus, this junior high Greek-god superstar had his own pony. How was I supposed to compete with that?

Thankfully, an instructor came and helped me on to the horse, because I had no idea how I was going to do it on my own. Sitting up there I felt very high, and when Star had swung herself easily into the saddle of her horse, we towered above everyone else.

In my mind we were a medieval king and queen riding out with the peasants. Star wore one of those pointy hats with veils fluttering out of it, and I was bedecked in shining armour.

And then the horse started to move.

Man alive, I thought they must have given me a camel by mistake. The thing swayed like a ship at sea – I swear I felt seasick.

I squeezed with my thighs to stop myself from falling off, and the bloody thing went faster. My shiny helmet – which was actually a dusty old riding hat – joggled about on my head and my bones rattled along the whole length of me. And people do this for pleasure? I thought.

We followed a bridle path that climbed up a gentle slope to begin with, and once I got used to the movement of the horse, and didn't feel at every step that I was about to fall off, I began to enjoy it. It was another hot day, but there was a slight breeze and we all had bottles of water in our saddlebags to drink. The path climbed some more, and the views were breathtaking. We could see mountain peaks rising on our left, and forests and meadows to our right. The shiny glint of streams or lakes flashed like signal lights as my eyes scanned the horizon. The horses climbed up a steeper stretch of path, and through a rocky streambed. I had to lean forward in the saddle to counteract the angle of the horse's body as it stepped over wet rocks and stumbled sometimes as its hooves slipped.

We reached a plateau and stopped for a picnic.

The horses were tied loosely to a picket fence and given water and nosebags of oats, and then allowed to graze or just stand around while we ate and lazed about.

Star and I ate with Natalie and Matt as well as Jack and Arash and Ashley and Shelly.

Mark and Eoin sidled up to us and started to sit down.

'You're not invited,' Matt said.

'Oh, I'm sorry,' Mark said, sarcastic as ever. 'Is this area reserved for the Romeos and Juliets in their budding teenage romances? How sweet.'

'Yeah, it is,' I said. 'So you've got no chance of joining in, have you?'

'Oh, I don't know,' Mark said. 'I think the girls prefer men to boys, isn't that right?' He directed that question towards Shelly and Ashley, but they just gave him withering looks.

'See,' he said, 'they're speechless with desire.'

Eoin laughed at this, which I thought was rich since he virtually never speaks either.

'So,' Mark went on, 'how's the code-breaking going? Still playing your little games?'

'What's it to you?' Arash asked, probably still upset about Mark teasing him about his Scrabble skills.

'Nothing, I couldn't care less. Still, I'm looking forward to Captain Bud's next barbecue – mmmmmm.'

With that he laughed and went away, trailed as ever by Eoin.

The girls asked us what he meant about Captain Bud's barbecue, so we told them all about the conversation around the campfire the previous night. In daylight, sitting in a meadow of flowers and butterflies, the whole thing seemed a lot less scary or believable. Still, it added weight to the rumour of the missing campers, even though it didn't really answer any of our questions.

- Eight -
Ten Paces North

The next day was Monday, so back to the normal camp routine. In the afternoon we had fishing, which was like something out of *Huckleberry Finn*. I couldn't believe they expected us to catch anything with nothing but bits of fishing line with hooks tied to one end, and the other end tied on to big sticks. They gave us live worms to spear with our hooks, which was totally disgusting, not to mention cruel. I bet Mark loved it. I was beside Natalie in the queue for collecting worms. She followed me back to where I'd left my stick and sat down beside me.

'It's pretty cool this camp, isn't it?' Natalie said, after a couple of minutes of sitting together.

'Yeah,' I agreed. 'Who'd have thought that after all these years of not seeing each other we'd be sitting together by a lake in America, fishing? It's weird.'

'Yeah.' Natalie laughed.

'I wrote and told my mum about meeting you again – you know, on Sunday when we had to write letters home. Remember how my mum and your mum used to be friends?' As soon as I said it, I wished I hadn't. Typical me, just open my mouth and spout rubbish without thinking about it. Natalie's mum was dead – or missing. Why did I have to bring her up?

'Yeah,' she said, 'my mum was always telling me about how you and I were born on the same day, and she met your mum in the hospital, and then they didn't see each other again until you and I started being friends. It's like we were twins separated at birth.'

'Yeah.'

We sat in silence for a little while, and then Natalie said, seemingly out of the blue, 'I don't live with my aunt and uncle any more.'

'Don't you?' I said, not sure whether to sound too interested, in case she didn't want to talk about it.

'No. It didn't work out.'

'Oh.'

'I live with my grandparents now. They're pretty old.'

'Are they?'

'Yeah.'

We stared at our lines, in case any giant fish had decided to grab the bleeding worms and get themselves caught. They hadn't.

'Do you ever see your real dad?' I said. Why couldn't I learn to keep my mouth shut?

She looked surprised for a moment, as if she didn't think I knew that Mr Anderson wasn't her real dad.

'No,' she said. 'I don't have a real dad. I mean, he died when I was little. I don't even remember him.'

'Oh,' I said. 'I'm sorry. I didn't know.'

93

Natalie's line started to jiggle, which gave us a moment's excitement, but it turned out it had just got caught in some pond weed.

'Hey, look, I caught a fish!' someone shouted. We looked up and saw Matt coming towards us grinning proudly and holding a dripping, flapping silver fish out at arm's length on the end of his fishing line.

'Cool!' said Natalie. 'What are you supposed to do with it now?'

'I don't know,' said Matt. 'Throw it back, I guess. But not before I've shown it to everyone.'

He was off again, showing off his catch to the other kids sitting about fishing. We could hear various responses, from admiration to horror, at the sight of the slimy, gasping fish.

'He likes to be the centre of attention, that boy,' Natalie said, watching Matt doing the rounds.

'Yeah,' I had to agree. I mean, it's true, but I felt a bit disloyal all the same. I am supposed to be Matt's best friend. But then Natalie is his girlfriend, so maybe it was okay to slag him off in front of her.

'Oh, guess what?' Natalie said, when Matt had ambled out of sight. 'I found another clue!'

She took a piece of paper out of her pocket and showed it to me. My first thought was, why wasn't it in our cabin? The first two clues were, and I just expected that they all would be.

'Where did you find it?' I asked her.

'Um, it was in my cabin – last night, when we went to bed. Look.'

I scooted closer to Natalie to look at the paper she held.

```
   CDO   SEEN   OYY   NSTTD   WAA   RWEH

HTBT   CNT   BEINA   NOPHO   OX   IEHLA

 ED   HOLEO   EATOO   EZTU   NDCRE   RKL

 HEISORNT   FLTD   WEU   KSLEX.
```

'It'll be the keyword cipher for SUNFLOWER,' I said. 'Did you count the letters?'

'Yes,' she said. 'There are ninety letters, which means, since the keyword had nine letters, we have to make a grid of nine columns and ten rows – eleven if we want to write the keyword at the top.'

'We should write out the message again in groups of ten letters first,' I said, 'and then we can write them down the columns in the right order.'

Natalie took a pen and paper out of her pocket, but instead of using them to write down the letters, she cradled them in her lap and said, 'Who do you think is sending these clues?'

I was impatient to get going on solving the code, and felt a bit irritated by her question. We'd already talked about it on Saturday before the sleep-out, and I told her then that I didn't know.

'If you think about it,' I said, to humour her, 'it has to be someone in camp planting the clues, because if a total stranger was wandering about posting things into cabins, someone would notice. It's a game, that's all. A bit of fun.'

I think I really did believe that at the time, or at least I wanted to. Because it *was* fun. Even the hints of danger and mystery were fun – because nothing really bad had happened, not yet.

'It's not like working out codes could do us any harm,' I said. 'It's not like the clues told us to go off into the woods in the dead of night or something, is it?'

Natalie smiled. 'You're probably right,' she said.

She started counting out groups of ten letters and writing them in rows.

Then she drew out a grid that was nine by eleven, and wrote the word 'SUNFLOWER' into the boxes in the top row.

'Hey!' said a voice behind me moments later. I recognised the voice, and she sounded more than a bit put out. 'Are you guys working on a new clue without the rest of us? No fair.'

It was Star, on her way back from kayaking.

'Hi,' I said. 'Natalie found this clue in her cabin. We were just . . . I mean, fishing is really boring, and we were . . .' I wondered why I was trying to make excuses. I didn't think we were doing anything wrong. Why shouldn't Natalie and I work on the clue together? After all, we were the ones with the code-breaking experience. I was just about to say something defiant, when Star crouched down and picked up the clue, as well as Natalie's bits of paper she'd been writing on, before either Natalie or I could stop her.

'We'll talk about it with everyone after dinner, all right?' Star said. 'I have to go now. You two are bound to have something else to talk about, right, since you're such old friends and everything.' With that she stormed off. For a moment I forgot to be annoyed at her, because the way her hair fanned out around her as she made her dramatic exit made my heart race, but the image was shattered by Natalie muttering, 'What a prat.'

I felt I should defend Star, and said weakly, 'Hey, that's my girlfriend you're calling a prat.'

Natalie jumped to her feet, almost knocking over her fishing rod, and yelled, 'FINE! I'LL NOT INSULT YOUR PRECIOUS GIRLFRIEND!' and stormed off in much the same way Star had.

At the time all I could think of was how Natalie's hair didn't fan out as impressively as Star's did.

After dinner the air was tense between me and Star and Natalie. Matt seemed a bit off with me too, so I figured Natalie must have said something to him. Everyone else just crowded around to look at the clue, oblivious to the undercurrent.

Natalie started to explain to everyone about how she'd found the clue, and how it had ninety letters, so she had started to draw out a grid with nine columns and eleven rows. She tried to take the paper back from where Star had laid them out, but Star was too quick for her.

'No, let me do it,' Star said. 'I want to see if I can remember everything that Luke told me last week about these keyword codes.'

'Sure,' said Natalie, with a saccharine smile.

Star took the grid that Natalie had drawn, and the numbered rows of letters.

'Now, if I remember right,' she said, 'you number the letters in the word "sunflower" alphabetically, like this.'

She wrote numbers over the grid.

'So, the first group of ten letters you write down the column under the letter E, right?'

Everyone watched while Star wrote in the letters:

'So the second row goes under F, and the next row goes under L . . .' Star worked away, and soon had the whole grid filled in:

7	8	4	2	3	5	9	1	6
S	U	N	F	L	O	W	E	R
T	H	E	N	E	X	T	C	L
U	E	I	S	H	I	D	D	E
N	I	N	T	H	E	W	O	O
D	S	A	T	T	H	E	S	E
C	O	N	D	B	L	U	E	A
R	R	O	W	T	A	K	E	T
E	N	P	A	C	E	S	N	O
R	T	H	A	N	D	L	O	O
K	F	O	R	T	H	E	Y	E
L	L	O	W	B	O	X	Y	Z

Star's writing was strangely wriggly – almost like runes. It looked odd beside Natalie's plain blocked letters.

'Hey, look,' said Arash, 'you can read across it now, from left to right: "then" – no, "the" – "next . . . cl . . . clue . . ."'

It was pretty easy to read the clue once it was correctly placed in the grid, even in Star's strange handwriting. It said:

THE NEXT CLUE IS HIDDEN IN THE WOODS.
AT THE SECOND BLUE ARROW TAKE TEN PACES
NORTH AND LOOK FOR THE YELLOW BOX.

We hadn't taken the blue hiking trail yet, but we knew the spot in the woods where all the trails began, so finding the second blue arrow would be simple enough.

'In the woods . . .' Ashley said in a worried tone, voicing out loud what I was starting to think. I remembered what I had said to Natalie earlier – 'It's not like the clues told us to go off into the woods in the dead of night . . .' Okay, I thought, so this clue didn't say anything about the dead of night, but still, if the clues were being sent by someone bad, someone who was trying to lure us away for some horrible purpose, wouldn't that be the perfect way to get us to go wandering alone in the woods? To say the next clue was hidden there?

'There's no way I'm going off into the woods,' Ashley continued. 'Even if the clues aren't being sent by some mad kidnapping murderer, the woods aren't safe anyway – there are bears and coyotes. I say we ignore it.'

'No way!' Marco said. 'This is like classic treasure-hunting. Take ten paces north – man, I love it! There's gotta be treasure with clues like that. I say we go and check it out.'

'What do you think, Star?' I said, trying to get back into her good books after what happened earlier.

'We can't ignore it!' Star said. 'That would be like throwing away our spirit of adventure. We've got to see this through to the bitter end, no matter what. I say we check it out.'

The pros and cons of going into the woods in search of the next clue were argued over the table, and by the time Captain Bud told us to go to bed, we were still split. We decided to discuss it again in the morning.

I went to bed that night not knowing that my life was about to be turned upside down.

- Nine -
MISSING

At breakfast I didn't see Star. I asked Shelly where she was, and she said that Star wasn't feeling well and was staying in her cabin for the morning.

Ah well, I thought, perhaps it's for the best if Natalie and Star are kept apart for a while, before they actually have a cat-fight. I remember wondering why girls couldn't just get along with everybody, like blokes did. That was before I found out that Star had gone missing.

Star had stayed in her cabin that morning because she'd said she wasn't feeling well, but then when the other girls went back between activities, she wasn't there. They didn't think too much about it because they figured maybe she'd gone for a walk or a shower or something. She didn't show up for lunch, but again we didn't think that was so strange if she wasn't feeling well. At the time I did feel uneasy about it – I tried to go and see her between activities, but boys are not allowed in the girls' cabins and Mrs Doris Bud was wandering around when I snuck over to them, so I had to give up. I didn't even get a chance to talk to the girls from her cabin after lunch because they all rushed off to some activity. I wish with hindsight that I'd made more of an effort to voice my worries, that I'd got people to pay attention to me and look for Star sooner. As it happened, it was dinnertime before everyone finally realised that nobody had seen her all day.

Shelly rushed back to check their cabin again, and called out for Star all around the girls' shower block and toilets. When there was no reply, we all agreed that Shelly should tell their cabin counsellor, Brandy (the nature studies teacher). Brandy instantly took the situation seriously, and she went and told the other leaders. Dinner was over by then, and some people had wandered off. A crackly loudspeaker system that we hadn't heard before called everyone back into the dining hall, and when all the kids had returned, Captain Bud started questioning everyone about when and where they had last seen her. Then we had to search the camp.

Everyone got paired up and told where to look, so nowhere got missed. Matt and I went to the hiking shed. We called for Star, and looked all around, but there was no sign of her. Matt was fiddling with the backpacks – looking inside them and counting them – and I snapped at him that she was hardly going to be inside a bag, was she?

'No, obviously,' he said. 'Shut up, will you? I'm trying to count. Yeah, I'm pretty sure one of these bags is missing. There were twenty-five bags, twenty-eight water bottles, thirty-one compasses, twenty-seven maps, and thirty whistles. One of everything has gone.'

'How do you know how many of everything there were?' I asked him.

He looked at me, exasperated. 'I count things, okay? It's a habit. Don't you?'

'Well, no,' I said. 'Not really.'

'I'll have to tell Natalie,' he said sarcastically. 'Yet another thing that'll make her prefer you to me.'

Matt's comment about Natalie seemed to come right out of the blue and for a moment I was tempted to challenge him about it, but I decided to let it drop – it wasn't the time for fighting with Matt.

'I bet she went looking for the clue.'

'What – Natalie?'

'No, moron – Star,' Matt said, rolling his eyes. 'Star is missing, right,' he said patiently, 'and so is a hiking bag with water, a map, and a compass, yeah?'

'Yeah, but . . .'

'Don't you remember last night she said that thing about not squashing your adventurous spirit or some-thing like that? Going off on her own after the clue is just the sort of thing Star would do, don't you think? She probably thought it was her destiny or something, or that she has magical treasure-finding powers. You know what she's like.'

It did sound plausible. Star was not the kind of girl to hide from danger. But if she did follow the clue, why had she not come back? It didn't sound like it was too far from camp. The second blue arrow – that couldn't be far into one of the hiking trails.

'Let's look for her in the woods,' Matt said.

'What? Are you crazy? We think Star went off into the woods this morning and something happened to stop her from coming back, so we should blindly go after her in the dark without telling anyone. Yeah, great idea.'

'She probably just fell and broke her leg or something,' Matt said. 'She's probably lying hurt in the woods wishing someone would come and rescue her. Don't you want to be that someone?'

'But it's so dark we wouldn't be able to see her.'

'We'll bring torches.'

'Shouldn't we tell the leaders?'

'Do you want to be a hero or what?'

It was pretty dumb, I know, but I agreed to go with Matt into the woods to look for Star.

The hiking shed was, logically enough, right beside the woods where the hiking trails began. Turning on our torches, we crept into the woods, making beams of yellow light that tunnelled between the trees.

'Here,' Matt said. 'Here's the beginning of all the trails, and the blue arrow points that way.'

I turned my torch on Matt, to see where he was pointing, and then on to the blue arrow to verify the direction. The arrow pointed off deeper into the woods, and we began to follow the path that stretched out in the direction that it indicated.

The path was narrow and littered with fallen twigs and branches. I was glad of the concentration required to walk without tripping and to look for the next arrow, as well as looking around for any signs of Star. Having something to think about stopped me from dwelling too much on the fear that was creeping up me like a clinging vine, threatening to immobilise me. Fear for Star, fear for myself. What was out there in the dark woods with us? An animal? A person? Had they already got Star? Would they get us next?

The swinging arc of my torchlight flashed on something blue. I brought the beam back and saw that it was the next arrow.

'Matt, look,' I said.

He jumped when I said his name, showing that he was as spooked as I was.

We'd remembered to bring a compass with us from the hiking shed, so we stood facing the blue arrow and looked to see which way was north.

We found north, and started pacing. One, two, three ... At ten paces we stopped and looked about us.

On the ground a yellow box glared at us, unmissably.

I picked it up and examined it. It was very light, made of something like balsa wood. The lid was stuck on with tape, and it looked like it hadn't been opened. I shook it and there was a noise which sounded very much like a folded-up piece of paper rattling around inside it. Star had not been there. We were the first to find the clue.

Matt and I looked at each other.

'She's not here,' Matt said, and his voice sounded shaky.

'We should get back,' I said, in an equally shaky voice.

'Yeah.'

Not opening the box, but bringing it with us, we turned around.

'Should we shout?' I said. 'In case she's nearby?'

'I don't know,' Matt said. 'If she's not here, then we don't want to be heard, by – well, you know, someone else.'

Or something else, I thought. Either way I agreed. We didn't want to be heard.

We stopped every few paces on the way back and swept our torches around, looking down the gaps between trees, searching for any sign of Star. I didn't admit to Matt that I was also checking for what might be hiding in the dark, although he must have been thinking the same thing because he too whirled around with his torch every time we heard a noise. Once or twice pairs of silver eyes shone back at us in the torch-light. Even with all the stopping, the walk back seemed to take less time. We quickened our pace as we came nearer to the edge of the woods, both of us eager to get back to the comparative safety of the camp.

When we stepped out of the woods, we both let out a sigh of relief. It was almost as if we'd imagined an aura of evil in the woods that lifted as we left the trees behind. Although, thinking about it, I realised that the whole camp could be covered in the same evil aura – we just didn't know.

'We should tell the counsellors about the missing bag,' Matt said.

I agreed, so we hurried back to the dining hall. Most people had returned from their searches already, and everyone looked worried, so we assumed (correctly) that Star had not been found. There were police vans parked outside the main cabin, and Captain Bud was deep in conversation with a man in a sheriff's uniform. We looked for Drew, to tell him about the hiking bag. When we found him, he was giving the sheriff and Captain Bud suspicious looks.

'Thick as thieves, those two,' he said, flicking his head to indicate who he was talking about. 'Everyone around these parts is living in each other's pocket. Go to church together, drive each other's kids to school, probably go hunting together. If Captain Bud's been a bad boy again, the sheriff is most likely in on it.'

We stared at him, speechless. Was he saying that Captain Bud had taken Star, and that the sheriff knew about it? Did he really mean that? It was like something out of a horror movie, where everyone in the whole town knows about the terrible thing that's going on, but no one will do anything about it. Surely the police could be trusted, though? This wasn't a movie, it was real life.

Why would Drew say it if it wasn't true, though?

Was it because Drew had done something to Star, and he was trying to scare us out of telling the police what we knew? Not that we knew anything. The only lead we'd had was the treasure-hunt clues, and it looked like she hadn't gone after the next clue after all. I had the box, still unopened, in my hand.

I backed away and Matt followed me. Drew didn't seem to notice us leaving; he still had his eyes fixed on Captain Bud and the sheriff.

Matt and I discussed what we should do. We didn't want to talk to either Drew or the sheriff, so in the end we went and told Arleen the hiking instructor about the missing bag, and she went to tell the other leaders.

Not long after that, everyone had returned from their searches, and still Star had not been found. We were sent to bed, but the counsellors stayed behind in the dining hall to be briefed by Captain Bud and the sheriff.

I went through the motions of getting settled – cleaning my teeth, putting on my pyjamas – without really paying attention to what I was doing. I felt strangely numb, or distant from what was going on around me. Matt told the other boys about us looking for Star in the woods, and finding no sign of her, and how the clue had still been where it said it would be. Then he told them about what Drew had said, and our theories of a horror-movie conspiracy.

The voices of the other boys in the cabin sounded wide awake and nervous.

'I know what you mean about it being like a horror movie,' KC said. 'I saw this movie one time – it was set in this little town in the mountains and everyone in the town was part of this big cult. They would rescue hikers and climbers who got stuck in the mountains, and then sacrifice them to Satan.'

'Do you think that's what happened to Star?' Tyler said.

'Don't be stupid,' said Arash, a little too loudly. 'It was just a film – that wouldn't happen in real life.'

'Something's happening, though,' said Jack. 'Do you remember Arleen the hiking instructor acting all sus-picious that day when you asked her about the missing campers, Luke? And Drew said that Captain Bud is good friends with the sheriff – that's very convenient.'

'What if all the counsellors are in on it?' Matt said. 'Even Arleen and Brandy. Even that smiley guy from the Squirrel cabin.'

'Man, I don't like this,' said Marco, his usual ever-present laugh now completely absent.

'If Star's disappearance is connected to the missing campers from three years ago,' Arash asked, 'then why did no one go missing last year, or the year before?'

'I know why,' KC said. 'They had to pace themselves – it would be too suspicious if kids went missing every year. They've been waiting years for this moment. Star might only be the first. There were three kids that went missing last time. Maybe there will be three again. Maybe two of us will disappear too.'

'Maybe they have a thing for smart kids. What if the clues are to whittle out the campers clever enough to satisfy them?' KC said.

'No, they couldn't be,' said Matt, 'because the clue in the woods was still there. We found it.'

We heard a noise outside the cabin then, as the counsellors were making their way back over, and all conversation ceased. Funnily enough, I don't remember Mark or Eoin joining in the discussion. Nobody said anything after Drew got back. We all pretended to be asleep, although I'm sure nobody was.

I hadn't joined in the conversation with the other boys – all the talk about conspiracies and sinister groups was just made-up rubbish. The only things that we knew were true were that Star was missing, and that a hiking bag had gone. Star told the other girls she was too ill to go to breakfast, and yet she was well enough to fetch a hiking bag (if it was her who got it), which made me think she had something in mind. But what? Why would Star go off on a hike on her own? Matt and I had ruled out her going after the clue. Yes, she was a free spirit, a rebel, but still, I couldn't believe she would just take off without telling anyone. She would have told Shelly, surely. Or me.

There was a jumble of emotions inside me that were almost too much for me to cope with – feelings of fear and worry and confusion. I was afraid to think about what might have happened, and what might happen still. I couldn't even allow my mind to picture the different possibilities. It was one thing telling stories about hypothetical kids from years ago but this was different. This was Star.

I felt worried that it was my fault, worried that there was something I should have done to stop her going off, to protect her.

And I felt confused. I'd only known Star for days – for less than two weeks – and yet she had turned my life around. She was different from any girl I'd ever met before – and she liked me, she fancied me. Did I love her? Would my world crumble if she didn't come back? Did my feelings go any deeper than her gorgeous hair and her great body and the way she always had something funny or interesting or startling to say? Did I want my feelings to go any deeper?

Inside me, bubbling up, were feelings I didn't like, feelings that made me feel guilty and dirty. I felt selfishly angry – it wasn't fair. I'd been having fun at camp, I was doing stuff I'd never done before, including snogging Star, and by getting lost and making us all afraid she'd taken these things away from me. If the camp was closed and we were all sent home, would I be more upset about losing Star or about losing my summer holiday?

With all those thoughts and feelings jostling around my head, I barely slept, and the bugle call in the morning seemed to take a long time in coming.

At breakfast we were told to stay within sight of two other campers at all times. Not that three kids would be much of a match against a whole village full of ritualistic killers, I thought.

I wrote all of our theories into my notebook – the same one in which I'd written about the sleep-out. That way if anything happened to me and anyone from outside the town came to investigate, they might find it and work it out.

We got a talk from the sheriff about safety and a call for anyone who had any information that might help them to find Star to come forward and tell them. Everyone was silent.

He said that the search and rescue crews were still out scouring the land around the camp, and that the forensics team were going to process the area around Star's cabin, so the whole of the girls' cabins were off limits to other campers. He added that he and the other police officers were going to stay around the dining hall, so if anyone thought of anything they might want to tell them, they should come and find them there.

Then Captain Bud stood up and said that our prayers were with Star, and that he was sure she was going to be found safe and well. He said that the best thing we could do to help was to carry on with the camp activities as normal, and not get in the way of the professionals who were giving their best efforts to getting Star safely back. I wondered if it was my imagination, or if he really did wink and smile smugly when the sheriff looked over at him.

It was virtually impossible to concentrate on anything all day. How were we supposed to learn how to tie knots, or the best way to light a fire, when we didn't know if Star was dead or alive? Even my first session on the rope course, which I'd been really looking forward to, passed in a blur. As I was walking across camp between sessions I overheard some girls complaining about not being able to go back to their cabins to get mosquito repellent. I wanted to scream at them for being so selfish, so insensitive. Star was lost and they were worried about bug spray?

In nature studies, Mark started asking the instructor, Brandy, all these questions about ferocious carnivores and poisonous plants that could kill someone out walking alone near camp, until the poor woman broke down in tears and had to go and get someone to cover for her. Mark and Eoin laughed out loud together when she was gone, and I was on my way over to them to punch Mark right on his evil face when (I guess, luckily) the counsellor who was covering for Brandy showed up.

It was Drew, who was in no mood for talking, and made us copy out the information from the laminated nature cards for all the remaining time.

In the afternoon, during horse-riding, I saw a car pull up in front of the main cabin. A man and a woman got out of the car, and then a girl who almost made me fall off my horse. I reined the horse to halt to get a better look, causing a bit of a pile-up behind me.

It wasn't Star, as I had first thought, but a younger girl who looked so much like her that it was almost unbelievable. The man and woman hurried into the cabin looking worried, and called the girl after them. It had to be Star's family. I wondered if their arrival meant Star had been found. No, I thought, they'd have been told she was missing. They'd have come anyway. Star was from New Jersey, a neighbouring state to New York, but still a few hours' drive away probably, judging by how long it had taken us to drive up the state from New York City.

The riding instructor shouted at me to move on, but still my eyes lingered on the door that Star's family had just gone through. Did they believe like me that Star couldn't be dead? That she was too vibrant, too bright? And did they like me fear that their belief was wrong and that death took no account of the brightness of the lives it stole?

I remembered when Natalie's mum and stepdad had gone missing. The coastguards and police looked for them for days, until they said it was too late to expect them to be found safely, and the search ended.

I wondered if it would be like that if Star was never found. Would life just go on from the point when she went missing, with us never knowing whether to hope or whether to despair? Is there a moment when hope dies and you accept that it's over? I prayed that that moment would never come for Star.

- Ten -
ON A KNIFE EDGE

After dinner everyone stayed in the dining hall. The hum of conversation was as loud as ever, but whereas usually it was interspersed with laughter, that night the laughter was absent. Minor arguments broke out in the tense atmosphere, but died away quickly as if people were afraid that their angry words would bring bad luck.

When we were finally told by Captain Bud to go to bed, people left the cabin in groups, huddled together for safety. Mark and Eoin didn't walk with the rest of the boys from our cabin, but when they passed us, Mark stopped and shone his torch in the direction of Matt's hands. 'If I was you, Luke, I'd check lover boy's hands for blood. My theory is that he finished off your girlfriend in a fit of jealous rage. I'd look out for Natalie now, maybe she's next. Unless he likes that little love triangle . . .'

'Shut up, Mark!'

Matt and I both turned on him, ready to take out our pent-up fear and anger on him, never mind the fact that he and Eoin were both bigger and tougher than us.

'Steady, boys.'

We hadn't been aware of Drew walking behind us. For a moment I teetered on the edge of ignoring Drew's warning and going for Mark anyway. I felt the momentum of my urge to fight almost too strong to deny. Drew pulled his knife out of his pocket and casually started cleaning dirt from under his fingernails with the point of the blade, while watching us quietly.

I felt tears of anger and frustration sting my eyes and I was glad of the darkness to hide them. The moment of indecision seemed to last for ever, but finally I barked out a swear word and turned my back on Mark and walked on. Matt followed me, and I heard Drew tell Mark and Eoin to wait with him for a moment to let us get a bit of distance from them.

For the second night in a row, sleep was far from me. How could I sleep when I didn't know where Star was? Maybe she was already dead. Maybe she was alive but someone was hurting her. I felt useless, crippled. I wanted to run out into the night and let my instinct lead me to her. I knew that search and rescue teams were working round the clock and that realistically there was nothing I could do to help them, but that didn't stop me wanting to.

In the morning we went to breakfast hopeful of hearing good news – surely Star would have been found in the night. But there was still no news. It was two whole days since Star had been seen. I knew what they say on the news when someone goes missing, that the more time passes the less likely it is that they'll be found alive, but I couldn't believe that Star could be dead. It was too surreal, too terrible. One minute she'd been there, filling the camp with her presence, the next she was just gone. Her story couldn't end like that. Could it?

Camp activities still continued. I did what the instructors told me without caring if I made it to the top of the climbing wall, or if my arrows hit the target. In fire-building, when I was in the woods gathering twigs, Natalie came up to me.

'Are you all right, Luke?' she asked, taking my hand. 'Are you coping?'

What could I say? That I felt like I was trapped in the middle of a bad dream. That part of me was sure I would wake up and it would all be over.

'I don't know,' I said. 'I . . .'

Before I could say any more an angry voice interrupted me:

'Oh, typical!'

We hadn't heard Matt coming towards us. He was standing with an armful of twigs looking at the two of us. 'You didn't waste any time, did you?'

Our hands were still joined, and I went to pull away, but Natalie gripped my hand more firmly.

'What? I can't believe you, Matt!' she spat back at him. 'I'm comforting my friend whose girlfriend is missing. Have you got a problem with that? Have you?'

Matt looked like he was balancing on a knife edge between guilty embarrassment, and indignation at finding me hand in hand with his girlfriend.

'Fine! Whatever.'

We watched him stomp off, and then our hands fell apart. I was on the brink of apologising to Natalie about Matt when she beat me to it.

'Sorry about him,' she said. 'He's an idiot sometimes.'

'I guess we're all feeling tense,' I said. I remembered what Matt had said when we were looking in the hiking shed for Star, something about there being another thing to make Natalie prefer me to him. The idea of Matt being jealous of me seemed crazy – he was so good-looking, all the girls fancied him, whereas I'd never had a girlfriend in my life before Star. Besides, I really didn't fancy Natalie – we were just old friends.

'His brother's sick, you know, back home,' Natalie said. She had a habit of saying things like that out of the blue. 'His little brother – he's got leukaemia. He told me about it one time when I was saying how terrible it was for you to be diabetic. It was like he was trying to compete with you, like his problems were worse than yours so I should give him all my attention. I don't know why I'm still going out with him,' she said. 'He's always trying to come between you and me.'

I started to feel a bit worried. What did Natalie mean by Matt coming between us – did she want us to be more than just friends? When we were kids I always thought of Natalie as one of the boys. She wasn't girly at all – she didn't play with dolls or wear dresses. Instead of Barbies her bedroom was usually filled with engines or radios from her stepdad's boat that she'd taken apart and was in the process of putting back together again. She'd changed a lot since then – her hair and figure now definitely made her one of the girls, and pretty gorgeous at that — but I still thought of her as the tomboy she used to be. Plus my head was filled with thoughts and feelings about Star; I could barely deal with getting through the days myself without worrying about someone else's feelings as well.

'We should get back,' I said, and turned to carry my wood back to the campfire.

I tried to keep out of Natalie and Matt's way as much as I could after that. Once or twice Matt looked like he wanted to talk to me, but I always looked away, or even walked away, from him when he did. Finally after dinner he cornered me.

'I'm sorry about before, mate,' he said.

'Yeah, don't worry about it,' I told him. 'It's nothing.'

'You must be pretty worried about Star.'

'Yeah.'

I was still looking for a way to get away from him when he started to tell me about his brother.

'We were really worried one time that my little brother was going to die,' he said.

'Natalie told me your brother was sick.'

'She told you?' For a moment Matt looked like he was going to get angry again, but then the moment passed. 'The point is, we all thought he was going to die, we were acting almost like he already was dead, you know, but he didn't die. He pulled through and went into remission, and he could get all the way better, and we realised we were wrong to give up hope. Sometimes things turn out okay, in the end.'

I knew Matt was trying to make me feel better, and I appreciated it, but I still wished he would just leave me alone. But he didn't leave me alone – he went on talking:

'I think the reason I've got so annoyed at you about Natalie is, well, if I'm honest, I get really fed up about all the fuss over my brother Simon. Since he got sick it's like I'm not even there any more. My parents are too busy worrying about Simon or going to the hospital with him, they've got no time for me. I know it sounds terrible – he could die and I'm worried about not getting enough attention – but it's no fun being the one who's not sick either. And then when Natalie started going on about poor Luke with his diabetes, well, it was like Simon all over again. Have you ever wondered if that's why your brother Ryan acts like such a jerk around you – because being diabetic makes you the special one that your parents worry about and fuss over?'

He didn't pause for me to answer, and I don't know what I'd have said if he did.

'Anyway, it's not your fault that you're diabetic, any more than it's Simon's fault that he's sick. It's my problem and I've got to deal with it, so I'm sorry. Okay?'

'Sure. Okay.'

Some things about Matt made more sense to me now, like how he seemed to get mad at me for no reason, or how he was never that interested in my diabetes, and how he always seemed to wander off if I was talking about it to someone. It had honestly never occurred to me that anyone would feel jealous or overshadowed by my illness. I'd never looked at my diabetes from other people's point of view — not my brother's or my friends'. I guess I'd been too wrapped up in myself.

I suddenly felt really tired. After two nights of not sleeping well, and then all the emotion of the past days, I thought I might just drop to the ground from where I stood.

'I'm going to bed,' I said.

'Right,' said Matt. 'See you.'

I walked to the cabins with some other boys who were heading that way, and I was asleep before anyone came back to our cabin.

- Eleven -
GOODBYE STAR

In the morning of the third day after Star went missing, we spotted a commotion outside the main cabin on the way to breakfast and rushed over to see what was happening.

Star's family were standing with Captain Bud and Doris staring over towards the woods by the rope course, so we turned and looked that way too. Official-looking people in uniforms were talking on two-way radios, and other people were milling about carrying medical equipment.

I saw the hedge that marks the boundary of the camp rustle first, then a man wearing the uniform of a search and rescue volunteer strode out from between the branches, followed by another volunteer holding the front end of a stretcher. Once out of the woods, he and the man holding the other end did something that made wheeled legs drop down from the stretcher so they could wheel it like a trolley across the grass. A figure wrapped in a blanket was strapped to it. Her honey-coloured hair spilled over the end and trailed behind them like a pendant. A plastic mask was held to her face with elastic straps, and a fourth volunteer was carrying a canister labelled 'O$_2$ – Oxygen'.

I wanted to run to her, but my legs wouldn't move. Star's parents and sister flashed past my eyes as they did run to her. The people holding medical equipment rushed over too. They allowed Star's mother only a second to hold her hand before asking her to step back, asking everyone to step back, to get out of the way, and wheeling Star to the infirmary where the door swung shut behind them.

The silence that followed the slamming of the door was like the whiteness of a fresh cut that lasts for only a moment before blood rushes in.

'Was that Star?'

'Was she alive?'

'Was she hurt?'

'Was there blood?'

Questions filled the air as more people swarmed to the scene.

'Did you see her?'

'Where was she?'

'Is she okay?'

So many questions.

'Time for breakfast,' said Captain Bud. 'Nothing more to see here. Come inside everyone.'

I flocked through the door with the others, as compliant and unthinking as a sheep. I collected porridge from the hatch in a daze and only half-heard Captain Bud telling us that Star was alive, but that he couldn't really tell us any more than that at present. The same questions that everyone had been asking were barging into my consciousness, battering my brain so it felt actually sore. Is she really alive? Is she hurt? What happened? Is she going to be okay?

The door to the cabin opened, and everyone's eyes turned that way. The girl who I'd seen arriving with Star's parents was standing there, looking in. I got to my feet and rushed over to her before anyone else could.

'Are you Luke?' she said.

'Yes.'

'Kathryn's awake. She's asking for you.'

I left my porridge uneaten, even though I knew I would pay for it later (damn diabetes) and rushed to the infirmary.

'What's happening?' Natalie called over to me, from her table near the door.

'Star's awake,' I said. 'I'm going to her.'

In the infirmary Star's parents were waiting outside the room that had been temporarily converted into a ward for Star.

'You must be Luke,' the mother said. 'Kathryn wrote us all about her handsome British friend. How nice to meet you.'

I was struck by the inappropriateness of her words. It wasn't exactly 'nice' to meet in these circumstances. But then, maybe things were better. Maybe Star (her parents called her Kathryn – typical parents) really was okay. I smiled and shook hands with the Hernandezes, but I was eager to get past them. To get to Star.

'Hi,' she said, smiling crookedly at me, her bruised face lying on crisp white pillows.

Her voice was croaky and weak, but still coloured with the wry humour I associate with her. 'I got a boo boo.'

I'd heard the other American campers use that expression; it meant a tiny hurt, like a cut finger or a splinter. Looking at Star I saw she had more than a 'boo boo'. Most of the bits of her I could see were bandaged and the side of her face was grazed black and red.

'They're airlifting me out of here,' she said. 'We haven't got much time, the helicopter's on its way.'

Her eyes flicked to the left and the right, as if she was checking that no one was listening, and then she beck-oned for me to lean in closer to her.

'I got another clue,' she said.

'What?' I was confused. Didn't Matt and I check the woods? Didn't we find the clue untouched?

'On Monday evening after dinner, when I went to bed, I found a clue under my pillow.'

'Under your pillow?'

The fact that Star was following a clue when she went missing changed everything. When Matt and I found the clue in the woods we were convinced that the treasure hunt had nothing to do with Star's disap-pearance, but we were wrong. Plus the clue was under Star's pillow, not just on the floor. The thought of the mystery clue-sender actually going into Star's cabin and knowing which was her bed creeped me out big time. They weren't necessarily going after Star, I reasoned –

they might have picked a random bed, but why? Why not just push the clue under the door like they'd done with the others?

'It's time to go now, Kathryn honey,' Mrs Hernandez said, leaning her head around the door to the room. 'Say goodbye to Luke.'

'Mom, no! I need longer to speak to Luke.'

'Kathryn, the helicopter's here, and we need to get you to hospital. I'll give you one minute, and then that's that.'

She closed the door behind her, and then Star leaned over to her bedside table, wincing painfully as she did. She opened the drawer and lifted out a piece of paper that she'd hidden under a book.

'I was following the clue,' she said as she passed me the paper. 'I fell into a cave, or I might have been pushed, I'm not sure – I felt my ankle being grabbed but it could have been just a branch or something. I . . .'

Paramedics came into the room then and lifted Star on to another stretcher. 'I didn't find the chest,' she whispered as they did. 'I . . .' Her sentence was cut off again, by the paramedics asking her if her straps were comfortable. I followed them as they wheeled her out of the infirmary and tried to ask her what she had been going to say. What had happened to her? Where had she been for the last three days? In a cave? What cave? What did she mean, she didn't find the chest? How had she got so terribly injured and who had done it to her? As soon as we got outside, though, conversation became impossible; the noise of the helicopter blades whirring obliterated all other sounds. Star mimed writing with her hand on imaginary paper and mouthed words that looked like 'I'll write you'. I nodded and shouted, 'OKAY!' but she couldn't hear me.

Star's mum and sister were going with her into the helicopter. Star looked past them to me and her mouth continued to move, frantically trying to tell me things, but I couldn't make out the words. She was still looking at me and trying to communicate when they lifted her into the helicopter and closed the door after her.

As the chopper lifted slowly off the ground, the blast of wind from its accelerating blades sent clouds of dusty dirt flying up into the air, making my eyes smart and fill with tears.

'Goodbye, Star,' I said, although nobody could hear me.

Star's dad had not got into the helicopter with the rest of the family – I guess he had to drive their car back home. He waved as he watched the chopper lift up and then turn and buzz away, reminding me of the dragonfly that I saw that day by the lake. Star's dad walked away then, but I stayed, my eyes glued to the shrinking form of the chopper until it flew out of sight. Watching my only ever girlfriend being taken away from me, and taking with her the answers to so many questions.

I had no idea what my timetable for the day was. I'd left breakfast before Drew had given out the printouts and I wondered what to do. I could see groups of kids about the place, doing archery or horse-riding or various other activities, but I couldn't see Matt, who as my buddy was always doing the same activity as me. I decided I may as well go back to the cabin until the break between sessions, when I could try again to find Matt. I started walking that way, and as I passed the shower block, I was struck by how empty and deserted the cabin area was when everyone was off somewhere else.

I stopped walking just before I reached the Chipmunk cabin and stood still, taking in the solitude. I turned slowly through 360 degrees. I couldn't see a single other soul.

Because of the way the cabins were clustered haphazardly, and because of their position in relation to the other camp buildings, there was effectively a big blind spot all around our cabin. I could hear in the distance the noises of people doing stuff, but it was muffled, as if the trees around the cabins acted as a soundproof barrier. I started walking again, and my steps sounded loud, my feet breaking twigs and kicking pine cones. For some reason I slowed down and stepped more carefully, almost on tiptoes. I paused by the door to my cabin and my heart almost froze. I could hear noises from within. Rustling and scratching that stopped as my foot hit the step, making it creak, but resumed when I stood still.

Someone was in the cabin.

There was only one way into or out of the cabin – the front door, where I was standing. If the phantom clue-sender was in our cabin and I walked in on him, what would he do? I still didn't know what had happened to Star, but I did know that she was following a clue that had been left in her bed, and that she was pretty beaten up.

Frozen in indecision, I couldn't move. I was torn between anger because of what had happened to Star, fear about what could happen to me, and just plain curiosity. I wanted to know what was going on.

The curiosity won and without giving myself too much time to reconsider, I pushed open the door and stepped inside.

Two small furry animals scurried across the floor. One of them was holding a small yellow packet from which shiny orbs were spilling and rolling across the floor behind it. The empty-handed one disappeared through a rough hole between the wall and the floor in the far corner of the cabin. The other stopped, dropped the packet – which I saw contained peanut M&Ms – cheekily picked up one of the spilled sweets between its two front paws, and then with a flick of its fluffy striped tail, disappeared after its friend. Chipmunks. The cabin's namesakes. I sank down on Matt's bunk, letting out my held breath in a chuckle.

'Man, you guys almost scared the crap out of me.'

I stood up then, and again my heart lurched as I saw a piece of paper lying on my bed. Had the clue-sender been in the cabin, and was it only by chance that I'd missed him? No, it was the printout of my timetable for the day.

When I met up with Matt later he was full of questions about Star. How was she? What had happened?

I felt as frustrated as Matt did by my lack of answers. I told him what I knew, though.

'Another clue? No way,' he said. 'Maybe Drew was

right and Captain Bud and the sheriff have set up this whole thing to lure kids away.'

I thought about that, but it still didn't make sense. If Captain Bud or the sheriff had attacked Star, why would they leave her hurt but alive? And why would they let her be found? Wouldn't she tell everyone what had happened, and ruin their plan for capturing more campers? 'Maybe they wore masks,' Matt said. 'Maybe Star fought back – she's pretty feisty, and Captain Bud's no spring chicken. Did Star not tell you *anything* about what happened?'

'She was starting to,' I said, 'but we hardly had any time. She only had time to give me the clue before they took her away. She said she'd write to me.'

'What does the clue say?'

Until Matt asked that, it hadn't even occurred to me to look at the clue. I took the piece of paper that Star had given me out of my pocket and laid it out on a tree-stump between me and Matt.

On one side was the original clue:

'It's a pigpen code,' I said. 'It's really old – the Free masons used to use it to pass messages. It's called a pig-pen code because . . .'

'Yeah, yeah,' Matt said, 'I don't want a lesson in the history of cryptology. What does it say?'

I turned the paper over. On the back Star had writ-ten out the key to the code: four grids with the alpha-bet filled into them in order.

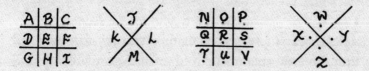

Underneath that she'd written the symbol for each letter, which represented its position in the grids.

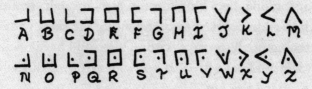

And finally she'd written the translation:

You're getting closer to your goal – adventure, wealth and pride. This clue will take you to a chest which you must look inside. Behind the barn the rope course looms, behind the rope course – treasure tombs. Happy hunting!

-Twelve -
CAPTAIN BUD'S OFFICE

That night there was a meteor shower forecast, and after dinner Captain Bud told us all to stand outside and watch the shooting stars.

The sight was pretty spectacular – hundreds of little streaks of light appearing and disappearing across the sky. I couldn't help thinking of Star, though, of how much she'd have loved to be watching the skies with us and telling us all to make wishes. If I could have made a wish it would have been to know the truth about what had happened to her.

After a while we went back inside and I got the rest of the gang together to show them Star's clue.

Matt must have been talking to the others, because by then everyone knew what I'd told him: that Star was covered in bruises and other injuries, and that she had hardly had time to tell me anything – only that she'd been following a clue and had fallen (or been pushed) into a cave.

I laid the clue out in front of them, and then turned the paper over to show them Star's translation.

'Treasure tombs?' said KC. 'That's pretty creepy. What do you think that means?'

'Maybe they just chose that word because it rhymes with "looms",' Arash said. 'It doesn't have to mean anything sinister.'

'It makes me think of Indiana Jones,' Marco said. 'You know, getting treasure from the cursed pharaoh's tombs.'

'Or that movie *The Mummy* – did you ever see that?' Tyler said. 'This evil mummy dude comes back to life and attacks these archaeologists.'

'Well, I think we can rule out Star being attacked by an evil mummy dude,' said Natalie.

'Something got her, though,' Tyler retorted. 'You don't get airlifted away in a helicopter for nothing.'

'Maybe,' I said, frustrated by my lack of knowledge. 'She was starting to tell me when they took her away. I wish someone would tell me what happened.'

Something made me look up then, and across the room my gaze took in Captain Bud, who was sitting by the fire with some of the other leaders. He was looking right at me, and for a moment our eyes locked. Then he abruptly looked away, and after whispering something to Mrs Bud, got up and left the room.

He knows, I thought. He must know. Even if he had nothing to do with what happened to Star (which I still doubted), he must at least have got the story out of her before she left. From what Drew had told us, Captain Bud believed in keeping unpleasant truths secret from us campers, but he couldn't hide the truth from me if I went to him and asked him outright, could he? I decided that's what I would do. In the morning, right after breakfast, I would walk up to him and get him to tell me once and for all what was going on.

When we were back in our cabin I told the other boys about my plan to confront Captain Bud. Everyone agreed that it was a good idea, and I was grateful when Matt said he would go with me.

When Arash warned us that Captain Bud is an anagram of 'pain' and 'abduct', Mark asked him if he knew any anagrams for 'shut up, idiot'. Drew came in before he could answer, and we all lay quietly in our beds waiting for sleep.

In the morning I went to breakfast still determined to confront Captain Bud. He stood up during breakfast and announced a talent show that was planned for Sunday afternoon – the next day – and pinned up a sheet of paper for people to sign up their acts. When Matt and I went over to him after the tables had been cleared, he said, 'Hello there, boys, you come to sign up for the talent contest? Sheet's just over there.'

'Um, no . . .' I said. My nerve almost left me as the camp leader sat at his table looking up at me expectantly, but then I thought again of Star and how badly injured she was and steeled myself to go on.

'I . . . we wanted to talk to you about Star.'

'Stars? What do you mean, son? You mean the meteor shower?'

Mrs Bud was listening in to the conversation, and she leaned over to her husband and said, 'He said "Star", honey. The Hernandez girl went by the name of Star.'

Captain Bud's genial expression instantly faded to be replaced by stony wariness. 'Kathryn Hernandez had an unfortunate accident,' he said, 'which wouldn't have happened if she had not disobeyed camp rules clearly stated in black and white in the camp literature. You know everything you need to know on the subject.'

'But I don't know anything!' I couldn't believe he could say I knew everything I need to know. 'What happened to her? What accident? Why won't you tell me? What are you hiding?'

I had raised my voice, and several people who had been milling around the talent show sign-up sheet stopped talking and turned to watch, eager to hear what would be said next.

Captain Bud seemed to be consciously controlling his breathing. His hands, which were resting on the table in front of him, squeezed into fists. I was struck by what a large and powerful man he was – his fists were huge and could easily have given Star her bruises and injuries. His skin was ruddy and tanned from spending lots of time outdoors, so when I tried surreptitiously to check his hands for signs of bruising, it was really too hard to tell. His knuckles were scuffed, with bits of ragged skin, but that could have been due to chopping logs or something. Mrs Bud put her hand gently on his arm in a restraining motion and said quietly, 'Remember, honey, calm inside and out.'

He twitched his arm, as if trying to shake off a bothersome fly, but he smiled at his wife anyway and said, 'Thank you, honey.' His eyes flicked up and took in the audience of interested faces. 'Why don't you follow me into my office?' he said to Matt and me. 'Doris, would you mind coming too?'

'Sure, honey.'

Matt and I exchanged glances as we followed Captain and Mrs Bud through a door I'd never noticed before beside the entrance to the kitchens. Captain Bud's office was fairly small and dominated by a large wooden desk. It also contained computer equipment and filing cabinets, and the wall behind the desk was decorated with the head and antlers of a large deer.

Mrs Bud sat down in an easy chair tucked into the corner of the room, and her husband sat behind the desk. Matt and I sat in the two remaining chairs, facing Captain Bud.

Captain Bud smiled, and his face seemed to take on a classic look of sympathy – too classic, like a mask worn by a politician to hide his true feelings.

'I understand your concern, boys,' he said. 'Your friend is missing for three days, and then she's found and whisked away from you so quickly – of course you're worried.' His smile widened. 'But there is really no need. Kathryn, um . . . Star is perfectly fine. Her family felt she would be better off at home after her ordeal – perhaps to give her time to reflect on the foolishness of her actions,' he chuckled, in the way parents do when discussing what their teenage children have been up to. I felt my anger not abating but rising inside me. I forced myself to stay outwardly calm, polite even.

'Captain Bud . . . sir,' I said, 'we would really like to

know what happened. Where was Star, and how did she get hurt? Could you tell us, please?'

Still smiling, Captain Bud answered, 'Of course. The girl wandered alone out of the boundaries of the camp to an area not covered by the hiking trails, precisely because of the dangers it contains. There are miles of unmapped cave systems around this region of the Adirondacks. Unfortunately Kathryn fell into one of them. Thankfully she was found by the rescue teams and tragedy was averted. The entrance to the cave where she fell has been cordoned off to prevent further accidents.'

The speech sounded rehearsed. I stared into Captain Bud's eyes as he spoke, looking for any sign of deceit. His face remained a mask, with only the slight twitching of one of his eyes betraying some inner emotion. Was it irritation? Was he worried about the reputation of his camp? Or was he hiding something worse – was his twitching eye due to fear that I would discover his guilt?

'Well, I'm sure you boys have an activity to go to.'

He was indicating that it was time for us to leave. He stood up, as if to further emphasise that the meeting was over. I had a ridiculous urge to kick him. Instead I stood up too, with Matt beside me.

'At least Star was found,' I blurted out, 'not like those other missing campers.'

Now Captain Bud's mask cracked and his face showed true rage. 'What did you say, boy?'

I kept my mouth shut, cowed by the anger in the face of the man who stood eye to eye with me but was much heavier.

'Well?' he pressed.

'Nothing,' I mumbled.

'Yes, nothing!' he said. 'The missing campers' – he used his fingers to indicate inverted commas around the expression, as if to belittle its validity – 'is nothing more than a rumour, d'ya hear? I will not have it bandied around that Camp Hope is not safe. If I hear anyone, anyone spreading that, that . . . hogwash, I'll, I'll . . .'

Mrs Bud now stood as well and walked over to her husband. To us she said, 'I think you'd better go now, boys. You've got your answer – Star fell. That's all.'

As we backed away out of his office, Captain Bud was still ranting, despite the efforts of Doris to calm him.

'What did you make of that?' Matt said as we hurried over to the rope course, where our first activity was based.

'I don't trust him one bit,' I said.

'Yeah, me neither,' Matt agreed.

We were late for our session on the rope course so we quickly got safety harnesses and helmets from the store room and helped each other to get kitted up.

If it hadn't been for everything else that was happening at camp, I would absolutely have loved the rope course. I'm not afraid of heights at all, and swinging from ropes between treetop-high platforms and balancing on rope bridges is brilliant – like being Tarzan, or one of Peter Pan's lost boys or something. Matt and I went around the course together, and between obstacles we tried to look out for the chest mentioned in Star's clue. 'Behind the rope course – treasure tombs,' it had said.

We looked down and around and could see a lot of the camp and surrounding wilderness, but no chest. We did see an area roped off with black and yellow tape that looked like what police use to seal a crime scene. 'Look,' I said to Matt, 'that must be the entrance to Star's cave.'

'Yeah.' His mind must have been going the same way mine was, because he said, 'It looks like a crime scene. Maybe the police don't believe Captain Bud any more than we do.'

We couldn't look for long, though, because the counsellors hurried us along to the final obstacle – an overhead pulley that you clung to and slid down a horizontal cable to land on a giant mat at the bottom.

I was completely knackered at the end of it – I had to get one of the counsellors to bring me a drink of Coke so I could get sugar into my system quickly. While I sat on the mat waiting for my blood sugar to rise again, I looked around some more for Star's chest. But again I couldn't see anything. It occurred to me then that we still hadn't looked at the clue that Matt and I found in the woods the night that Star went missing. Maybe it would have more information about finding the chest.

I brought the little wooden box with me to lunch, so we could look at the clue in the free time afterwards. As the clue-solvers gathered around our table the atmosphere was much different from how it had been on other occasions. There was no Star for one thing, and I felt her absence strongly. Everyone stared at the box in silence, and nobody made a move to open it.

I think it was Ashley who broke the silence. She said,

'If whoever is leaving clues is someone from camp, a counsellor say, and they don't mean us any harm, then why didn't they come clean when Star went missing? They could have told everyone to search by the rope course as soon as we noticed she was gone.'

Ashley had a point. This hadn't occurred to us on the night of Star's disappearance, because we'd thought then that she hadn't gone after a clue. But now that we knew she did, it put more questions in our minds. Did it mean that it was someone from outside camp leaving the clues, so they didn't know that Star was missing? Or did it mean it was someone inside camp, but that they did mean us harm?

'Shall we look at it?' I said.

Everyone nodded, so I picked the box up from the table and, like Indiana Jones unsealing some ancient artefact, I tore the tape around the rim of the lid and opened it.

I was almost expecting an evil spirit to rise like a mist out of the box, or at least a dazzling light or something. Instead the box just sat there, with the piece of paper we'd heard rattling inside it folded on the bottom.

I lifted it out.

When I unfolded the paper, I could see instantly what sort of code it was. Dots and dashes, separated by diagonal lines traced a border around the edge of the page, and were also written in the middle – Morse code. Natalie and I used to know it so well that we could talk to each other using only dots and dashes. I wondered if I could still remember it well enough to translate the clue.

— ·· /· /· — /— ·· /· /— · /— · · /· — · /· — /· /— · /· /· · · /· · · /

‐ /· · · · /· /· /· — /· — · /· — · /— — — /· · — · — · /

‐ /· · · · /· · /· /— — · /— — — /— — — /— — — /— · · /

— — /· — /— — /· · /· — /— — · /· · · /· · /· — · /— · · /

· · /· · · /· /— — /· · /· · · /— · · · /· — /· · /· — /— · /· /

— · — · /— · /· · /· — — — /— · ·

\· · · · \· · — \· \· \— · \· · · — \· — \— \· \· · — \— · \—· · \

It looked like two different messages: the one around the edge of the page, and the one in lines across the middle. A few people around the table recognised it as Morse code, but only Natalie, Arash, and I knew what the individual dots and dashes stood for. Arash had the idea of writing out the Morse alphabet, so everyone could join in translating the clue.

A ·— B —··· C —·—· D —·· E · F ··—·
G ——· H ···· I ·· J ·——— K —·— L ·—··
M —— N —· O ——— P ·——· Q ——·— R ·—·
S ··· T — U ··— V ···— W ·—— X —··—
Y —·—— Z ——··

While he wrote it, he told us that 'the Morse code' is an anagram of 'here come dots'.

Everyone started working out what the message said, and the first word we got, worryingly, was 'dead'.

Dead end, red herring, dead end, red herring.

Those two phrases were repeated around the outside of the page. Feeling a sinking sensation that the rest of the clue wasn't going to be much use to us either, we nevertheless set to translating the lines in the middle, and this is what they said:

The art of the good magician is misdirection.

This clue was a dummy. The instructions about following blue arrows and taking ten paces north were just to throw us off the scent. To keep us away from the real clue that Star had followed all alone to the outside of the camp beyond the rope course – where something happened to her to make her spend three days in a cave and come out covered in injuries.

We stared in silent disbelief at the words we'd written beneath the dots and dashes on the page.

Whoever was sending those messages was playing with us. But the question on all of our minds was: was it a game that could end in death?

- Thirteen -
LUCKY BEAR TOOTH

We were all nervous, all of us clue-solvers anyway. Everything about camp felt ominous. Even the other campers were coming under our suspicion, which didn't make sense since none of them could have been at the camp the last time kids went missing. Still, I kept imagining the other kids were talking behind my back, or looking shifty. Could it be that creepy-looking boy in the Racoon cabin sending the clues? I wondered. What's his name – Colin somebody? Or Mark and Eoin? Mark was evil enough, and Eoin just went along with everything Mark said. The counsellors looked even more suspicious to us now as well. I could easily imagine Drew stealing off into the woods and happily hacking a camper to bits – didn't he relish gutting those rabbits? And Captain Bud appeared more evil each time I looked at him.

It wasn't just a bit of fun any more. It didn't seem that Star's accident *was* such an accident. Why else would the clue-sender send us on a wild goose chase if not to give him the chance to get Star to go off on her own?

Matt and I didn't pay attention in fire-building when Drew was explaining how to build a log-cabin fire, so we had no idea what to do when it was time to build ours. Drew came over to me when I was furtively trying to copy Mark's fire. Uh oh, I thought, I've been rumbled. But Drew was not coming over to give me a hard time; instead he dropped something white that dangled from a leather string into my lap.

'There's your bear tooth,' he said. 'Don't say I never do nothing for you.'

I looked at the tooth, which to be honest I'd completely forgotten about. Drew had bored a tiny hole in it to accommodate a leather thong that he'd threaded through.

'Whoa, thanks,' I said.

'Any time,' he said, smiling back at me. I think it was the first time I'd seen Drew smiling when it wasn't a sarcastic sneer. The others looked between him and me in wonder and when he sauntered off, Matt said:

'If Drew is the mad murderer, you'll be all right. He obviously likes you.'

'Unless,' said Natalie, 'he *is* the mad murderer, and he's just being nice to you so we don't suspect him when you do go missing. If I was you I'd be worried.'

'What?' I said. 'Don't say that. You don't really think that, do you? Besides, nobody's been murdered, so there is no murderer, right?'

'Nobody except the infamous three missing kids,' Matt said.

'Three missing kids that might not even have existed,

from four years ago, when Drew wasn't even here,' I came back with.

'Which we know because . . . ?'

'Because he told us,' I said lamely. 'Okay, so we only have the word of our possibly psychotic cabin counsellor to go on about anything to do with the missing campers, except the rumour as passed on by Tyler's distant friend or relation, which really couldn't be relied on. But still . . .'

I put the bear-tooth necklace on anyway – it *was* pretty cool. I almost felt like I'd killed the bear with my bare hands, and wore his tooth as a trophy rather than just having happened upon it when digging in the dirt. Lost in my own imagination, I didn't notice what I was doing.

'Luke! Your trainer!'

'What?'

Natalie pointed wildly at the end of my foot, which I had absentmindedly pushed between the sticks in the wall of our log-cabin fire. Brown smoke that smelt of burning rubber was coming through the gap my shoe had made. I quickly pulled my leg back with a shriek and started jumping up and down before plonking my whole foot in the bucket of water with a satisfying hiss.

'The bear tooth'll give you good luck, Luke, but it won't make you invincible,' Drew said, this time smiling with his characteristic smirk. I was almost relieved to see it. See, I thought, he's not being nice to me now. He can't be planning to kidnap me, or else he wouldn't have made fun of me in front of the others.

There was another thunderstorm at dinnertime that Saturday. I couldn't help thinking of Star standing out in the rain the day of the first thunderstorm, looking like she owned the world.

Dinner was this kind of savoury rice with bits of onion and mushroom and meat and stuff mixed up in it. It was all right.

After dinner, the code-breakers discussed what we should do next.

We agreed that the clue in the woods was a red herring, which meant that Star was on the right track with her clue – except that she never found the treasure chest, because she fell down the hole.

'Maybe we should go to the rope course and look for the chest,' I said.

'Yeah,' said Natalie, 'except . . .'

'Except that whoever got Star might be lying in wait to get us,' Ashley cut across her.

'We don't know that anybody got Star,' Arash said. 'They probably didn't. Captain Bud said she just fell down. I'm not saying we should all trust Captain Bud, but it kind of makes sense, don't you think? If someone had made her fall, they would have gone down after her, it stands to reason – and if they had, then, well, I don't think she'd have been found alive.'

'I think we should look for it,' Matt said. 'What harm could it do? If a bunch of us go, then one bad guy, if he even exists, is hardly going to jump out on all of us, is he?'

Everybody thought about it for a while. We now all

wanted more than ever to know what was in the mysterious treasure chest. No one even brought up our theory that the whole camp staff, and even the whole of the nearby town, were in on the abductions. By not mentioning it, maybe we were hoping the possibility would just go away. It wasn't a trap to lure victims; it was a treasure hunt with a reward. A tiny voice in my head tempted me to go off on my own to look for the chest. Finders keepers. If I found it first, wouldn't the treasure be mine? I looked around the others, their faces going through different expressions, and I wondered how many of them were having the same idea. But I couldn't do that. We were all in this together, all for one and one for all. Besides, Matt was right in what he said about there being safety in numbers. I didn't fancy being alone anywhere around camp just in case I *was* being stalked by a madman.

'Yeah,' I said, 'Matt's right. We should all go together to the rope course.'

'But when?' said Natalie.

'What about right now?' Marco asked, always ready for some fun.

'No,' said Arash, the voice of reason, 'it's too dark; we'd never see a chest in the dark.'

'But in the daytime the rope course is out of bounds,' I said, 'unless you're there with a counsellor, and then how would we explain that we were off hunting for treasure instead of climbing up the rope ladders?'

'Hmm, we'll have to go some time when it's light, but when there aren't any counsellors about,' Natalie said.

'What about during flag-raising?' Matt asked. 'All the counsellors go to that, don't they? If just a couple of us, or three or four at most, go, nobody would miss us. We'd have to be quick, but maybe it's our best chance.'

We quickly agreed that it was a good idea, although it meant waiting until Wednesday before we could find the treasure. Still, these things take careful planning, we decided. It would be stupid to mess up now by rushing into things.

Once we'd settled in our minds that we would look for Star's chest the next Wednesday during flag-raising, it was like a weight lifted – for me anyway, and I think the others were more relaxed too. It seemed like we could forget all about it for a few days and get on with enjoying being at camp.

We played a game of consequences for a while then. The game where you make up a story on a piece of paper except everyone writes a different bit and you can't see what's gone before. You start with a girl's name, then that she met up with (boy's name) at some place. She said something, then he said something, and the consequence was … Some of them were really funny, or just completely crazy. It got pretty X-rated, though, so we had to throw them in the fire when we'd finished so the counsellors wouldn't find them.

I was sitting between Natalie and Ashley when we played. Ashley seemed more animated than usual and I found myself really getting along with her. We were laughing so much together over something Ashley had written that we didn't notice Natalie leaving. The game petered out, and Matt went off to do something with the other boys. I stayed talking to Ashley. I didn't fancy her – my feelings for Star were too strong and confused for me even to think about fancying another girl, but Ashley was pretty, and I had to admit I was enjoying her attention. When one of Ashley's cabin mates came along to ask her to come over to her table, she stopped and backtracked when she saw that Ashley was with me.

'Oh,' she said, 'you're talking to Luke. Right. I'll just, um, leave you to it then.'

Ashley blushed hotly, and mumbled something that might have been '*Shut up!*' to her friend. I looked between them, and then down at my hands. I didn't want to lead Ashley on, or encourage anything, but I felt flattered at the thought that she might fancy me. It was ironic, though, that for most of my life I hadn't been able to get a girl to look twice at me, and now that I was going out with Star, I was getting too much attention from girls. (Were Star and I still going out now that she'd left? I wondered, would I ever even see her again?)

Natalie came back then, and I was quite relieved that I wouldn't be alone with Ashley any more. Natalie didn't join us, though, but went over to the table with the rest of her cabin mates. She didn't even look at me when I called out to her.

Lots of people were practising acts for the talent show. I couldn't believe it! Why would anyone put themselves through the embarrassment? Marco and Tyler were doing a comedy duo. Evil Mark and Eoin were doing a mind-reading act. Lots of girls were singing solos (I wondered if the camp shop sold earplugs), Natalie was writing a funny poem, and even Matt was doing something – acting out some lines from Shakespeare. Ashley went off to practice singing with some other girls, and since I wasn't planning on performing, and so had nothing to practice, I just sat by myself for a while randomly watching people, and thinking about my time at camp.

I had noticed in kayaking that my arms were definitely less weedy than they had been before I came to camp. Ryan will have a bit of competition when I get home, I thought. My archery skills were improving too. I wish things could have been different. If it wasn't for what happened, coming to camp would have been the best thing that ever happened to me.

I got bored after about twenty minutes, and saw that Ashley had stopped singing and had gone over to sit at a table across the room.

Natalie was at the table too, scribbling things on a piece of paper with lots of crossing out and asking people to think of words that rhymed with 'buddies'. Matt was behind her, mouthing the words to his acting piece while strutting about and waving his arms dramatically.

Ashley was sitting beside Natalie, looking over her shoulder at the poem she was writing. I went over to her and said, 'Hi.'

'Hi,' she said. I knew there was something wrong the moment she spoke. She sounded worried or something. Her face was pasty-looking as well, and her forehead was creased with frown lines.

'Are you all right?' I asked her.

'Um, I feel a bit ill actually,' she said, looking up at me. 'Oh no, I think I'm going to . . .'

Instead of words, vomit erupted from her mouth, effectively finishing the sentence for her. As I was standing in front of her at the time, I got a bucketload of puked-up rice with bits splattered all over me.

'Ohhh,' she groaned, 'I'm sorry. Uh . . .'

There was more.

One of the counsellors rushed off for the camp nurse, who came quickly with water and a blanket for Ashley, and bundled her off to the infirmary.

I was left standing, watching her go and dripping regurgitated rice.

'Man, you stink,' Matt said, standing well back from me and holding his nose.

'Yeah. Well, I'll just go and get cleaned up then,' I said sadly.

Ashley spent the night in the infirmary, although Natalie said she was feeling much better when she went to see her after breakfast.

At Sunday morning meditation time I had plenty of things to think about: my feelings for Star now that she was gone, my theories about what had happened to her, my theories about who was sending the clues, and what would happen when we went looking for the chest on Wednesday. The hour flew by and I felt just as confused at the end of it.

Then we had to write our letters home. I thought about writing to Star, but realised I didn't have her postal address. I figured I probably shouldn't go and ask

Captain Bud for it.

I wrote to my parents and told them about the rope course and the talent show. I didn't mention the clues and I didn't mention Star.

Ashley made an appearance at lunchtime, but at the sight of the grilled cheese sandwiches she started to turn green again, and said she'd maybe better go back to the infirmary for a bit longer after all.

The talent show began after lunch and went on for hours.

Matt's act was pretty cool. He acted out this poem from Shakespeare. Apparently he's in this Saturday morning drama school, and it was the piece he had to learn for his audition.

> All the world's a stage,
> And all the men and women merely players . . .

He got a standing ovation. I was kind of glad Star wasn't there – she'd have just about wet herself with delight over how 'British' he was.

Natalie acted out her poem as she recited it as well. She gave me a handwritten copy of it after the show, to add to my notebook. I thought it was pretty funny – especially the sting in the tail:

> Intelligence pays,
> At least this year it has done,
> My smarter than average buddies.
> The reward – well, we're here,
> Having fun in the sun,

Even hiking through fields that are muddy!
Camp life, how we love you, from
Leathercraft to climbing, to sleeping out
Under the stars (howwwlll!)
Every creature that lives here's my
Sister and Brother
(Except mozzies and coyotes and bears).
Now listen, you guys who I've come to admire,
Dear friends I don't want to forget,
Everybody come closer, and listen to me.
Ready? Good, now you're going to get wet!

From behind her back at this point she produced a giant water pistol and sprayed the first three rows in a huge wet arc. It was so warm in the crowded room that nobody minded getting wet, but the surprise did make a lot of people scream and jump up from their seats.

Marco was funny, even though a lot of his jokes were about American things that us British kids had never heard of.

Mark and Eoin did a mind-reading act. Mark wore a black cloak, made of a waterproof sheet that usually covered the mat in the rope course. I thought it suited him – made him look even more like an evil genius.

There were endless singing acts, and a smattering of jugglers and plate spinners. Some of the counsellors did a funny sketch, which mostly involved them squirting each other with ketchup and mustard. Naturally Drew was not one of them.

On Monday, I thought Wednesday seemed like a long way off, and I started to think that maybe we should go to the rope course earlier. What if someone else found the chest before then? Someone might stumble on it by accident: one of the counsellors, or even Evil Mark – he might have already found it when he was getting the black tarpaulin to use as the robe for his magic act. It would kill me, I thought, if Mark got to the treasure before us.

My mind was getting more and more preoccupied with where the chest might be. It had to be hidden well enough that someone wouldn't just find it accidentally, but not so well that it couldn't be found by someone following the clue. Star's clue was pretty vague: 'behind the rope course – treasure tombs.' I could barely force myself to wait until Wednesday.

Whatever was wrong with Ashley seemed to be contagious, because campers started dropping like flies. Matt threw up in abseiling. For once, thank goodness, I wasn't in the line of fire, but unfortunately for the four or five kids who were bouncing down on ropes below Matt, they were. He was in a really bad mood all day – he'd had a row with Natalie during fire-building, but he seemed to be healthy enough at lunchtime, because he'd eaten loads.

Another girl from Natalie and Ashley's cabin got sick too, and I saw Arash looking pretty green over breakfast on Tuesday. At this rate, I thought, there would be no one well enough to sneak off during flag-raising. At least I didn't seem to be affected, and Natalie was fine as well. It occurred to me that it might even work in our favour. If lots of people were sick, and we didn't show up for flag-raising, maybe the counsellors would just assume that we were puking up too and think no more about it.

- Fourteen -
THE TREASURE CHEST

On Tuesday night Drew was in a foul mood. I was already tense enough thinking about ditching flag-raising in the morning to follow the clue, so when Drew stomped into the cabin swearing and shouting I nearly jumped out of my skin.

'I want every one of you boys to empty your lockers,' he said. 'NOW!'

We opened the cupboards beside the bunks and started taking out our belongings and laying them on our mattresses. Matt and Arash were in the infirmary, so Jack and I emptied their lockers too. Drew paced impatiently while we did it, chewing on his knuckles and checking everyone's haul. When all the cupboards were empty he made us turn out our pockets. We shot furtive looks at each other, but nobody dared to speak.

'If I find one of you has taken my . . . I swear I'll . . . HOT DAMN!' Drew was ranting incoherently. 'Captain-you're-on-your-last-warning-young-Drew-my-lad-Bud would have my hide if he thought . . .'

Drew had obviously lost something important and

thought that one of us had taken it. His knife maybe? He probably wasn't supposed to carry a knife, so if he lost it and one of the kids hurt themselves or somebody else with it, he'd be in big trouble.

He looked around the cabin, running his finger through his long, lank hair so that it stood up at strange angles. His eyes took in the mayhem that his enforced unpacking had caused.

'Clear up this mess!' he ordered, before stomping back out of the cabin. He didn't go far, though – we could hear him stamping and huffing outside the cabin door. Not wanting to provoke his wrath any further, we quietly tidied up and got into bed. When Drew came back in we all pretended to be asleep.

In the morning it was only me and Natalie who went looking for the treasure chest. Several of the other code-breakers, including Matt, Arash, and Ashley, were still sick, and we figured somebody would have to show up for flag-raising or the counsellors would go ape and send out a search party or something.

I met Natalie behind the girls' cabins. It was the closest I've ever come to doing something forbidden and as I ran between hiding places on my way to our rendezvous my heart fluttered with guilty excitement. Nobody challenged me, or even saw me as far as I could tell, and Natalie was waiting for me when I arrived.

'Ready?' she said, and I smiled as I nodded back at her. I was reminded of when we were kids. We used to meet outside Natalie's house to walk to school together, and sometimes we would meet early, so we could stake out the area for enemy activity – part of our ongoing spy game. Back then we'd known that it was just a game, even though we pretended to believe it wasn't. It was different now. If this was a game, then we weren't the ones making up the rules. The possibility of real bad guys hung over us and made everything more serious. I almost wanted to take Natalie's hand like I used to sometimes when we were little. But I didn't. Things were too complicated now. Instead we walked side by side to the beginning of the rope course.

'The clue said beyond the rope course,' I said, 'so I guess we should start looking at the end, by the aerial run.'

'Yeah,' Natalie agreed. 'Come on.'

Since Star's disappearance, a new security fence had been added to the hedge that marks the boundary of the camp. Ugly sharp razor-wire spiralled along the top of it. It reminded me of movies about people trying to escape from prisoner-of-war camps and getting shot as they attempt to scramble over the wires. There were no guard towers at the rope course, but still the wire looked out of place and threatening. We ignored it, though, as our eyes scanned the ground and the shadows beneath the wooden supports that held up the lofty platforms on the rope course. There was an equipment shed as well to be checked out, with some logs piled up behind it. In the distance we heard the wailing of the bugle which meant that the folded flag was being ceremoniously carried to the flag-pole, and which reminded us that we didn't have much time.

We split up, Natalie to the right of the shed, and me to the left. I was looking for anything that stood out – freshly dug ground, corners sticking out where there shouldn't be any – even something shiny, anything that might be a treasure chest.

After a few minutes of not finding anything, I heard Natalie exclaiming, 'Surely not!'

'What?' I said, going over to her and following her gaze down to the dark ground behind the logs.

On the ground was a tiny pink plastic box, shaped like a treasure chest. It looked like something that little sweets might come in.

'Do you think that's it?' Natalie said.

I looked at the tacky little box and felt like an idiot.

'I don't believe it! Some treasure chest.' I said, kicking the logs that the box lay behind. 'We might as well look at it, though – maybe it's full of really small diamonds.'

She laughed, and bent down and picked up the box, brushing crumbs of dirt off it with her fingers. The lid opened easily, and inside was not diamonds, but another piece of paper.

It said:

I think you'll find what you're looking for is quite beneath me.

I knelt down and scrambled in the dirt with my fingers, trying to find what was beneath the box. I was reminded of the day I found the bear tooth that now swung under my chin on its leather thong.

Nothing.

'Damn!' I yelled, kicking the ground in frustration. Kicking and kicking and kicking again − first with anger, but as realisation dawned I kept kicking just to hear the distinctly hollow echo that rung out from the earth below.

'Beneath me! The caves! Star's caves!' The words came out disjointedly, as I wanted to say them more quickly than I could think of proper sentences. I stopped kicking, and made myself calm down.

'The treasure is hidden in the caves beneath the rope course,' I said to Natalie. My eyes sank to the ground as if I could magically see through the layers of dirt and rock to the underground caverns, glinting with hidden treasure with my name on it. Now I did grab Natalie's hands, and instinctively, without thinking, I twirled her around. 'We've found it!' I said. 'It's in the caves.'

She laughed, catching my excitement and twirling me back until we both fell down on the ground giggling. I could have lain beside her for ages, our laughter an outpouring of our bottled-up hysteria, but I happened to glance at my watch and saw that it was past time for breakfast to start.

'Uh oh,' I said to Natalie, trying unsuccessfully to suppress my smile and look serious. 'Look at the time. We've got to go.'

We managed to slip into the dining hall unnoticed in the jumble of people fetching porridge and milk from the hatch. Only half the guys on my table were well enough to make it to breakfast − including, unfortunately, Mark and Eoin. I had to try to tell the others about what

Natalie and I had discovered in the moments when neither Mark nor Eoin nor Drew was at the table.

Bizarrely, Marco and KC were not as excited as me by the news.

'Man, are you nuts?' said Marco. 'Who'd be crazy enough to climb down the pot hole that almost killed Star because a piece of paper said to?'

I stared at him in disbelief. Marco had always been upbeat about the whole treasure-hunt thing, and he picked now to wuss out on me?

'I agree with Marco,' KC added. 'Going down there would be a bad idea.'

'Going down where?'

Mark had arrived back at the table with his steaming porridge.

'They found another clue that said the treasure was in the caves under the rope course,' Eoin said. I spun around and saw that he too was standing behind me, listening in.

'For crying out loud, keep your voice down!' I told him. 'Do you want the counsellors to hear?'

'Well, frankly, we don't give a toss,' Mark said, 'except that it might be fun watching you getting lectured.

'On the other hand, then we'd miss the fun of you hurting yourself on your little wild-goose chase, so actually, Eoin, do keep your voice down. Let the children play, and if it all ends in tears, at least we'll be able to laugh at them, so it won't be all bad.'

I glowered at Mark, determined to hold on to the high I'd felt with Natalie on the rope course, and not buy into his negative view of reality.

I couldn't, though. I hated the fact that he was probably right to throw cold water over my excitement. My
euphoria seeped away, to be replaced by irritation.

I was annoyed at Matt for being sick and not being
there for me. I was annoyed at Marco and KC for being
as downbeat as Mark. I was annoyed at Mark and Eoin
for eavesdropping and for always being so bloody mean
and sarcastic. The weather didn't help either. Another
storm was brewing and the humidity and heat sapped
my energy just like the mosquitoes relentlessly sapped
my blood.

The rain hung heavy in the clouds as I fumbled
through fencing, but didn't fall until half-way through
horse-riding. The instructor finished the session early,
but we still had to stable the steaming horses and put
away their saddles and bridles in the dripping tack
room. The sky darkened, but still the lightning was less
dramatic than it had been in the night-time storms.
Puddles formed quickly, and just as quickly the thirsty
earth soaked them up, only for the torrential rain to fill
them again. Reddish-orange mud like clay slick coated
our trainers as we ran to the shelter of the main hall, our
arms raised over our heads to give ourselves some pro-
tection from the weight of water that battered us.

Lunch was served early, and the steam that rose from
the sodden campers matched the steam that curled from
the bowls of hearty soup. Afternoon sessions were can-
celled, and everyone hung around in the dining hall,
watching the rain through the windows like Noah
through the windows of the ark.

I felt caged by the storm. I was still riled up and with no outlet for my anger I paced, ignoring invitations to join in games or conversations.

But then my mood changed as it occurred to me that the weather was in fact perfect – the perfect cover for getting to the entrance of the caves unnoticed. Who would miss me, I thought – or us? Natalie deserved to be in on this too; she hadn't abandoned me through sickness or apathy like the others had. Who would miss Natalie and me in the crowded hall with no organised activities?

Once the idea had come to me, I couldn't wait to carry out my plan. I quickly found Natalie talking to a group of girls, and pulled her aside.

'Let's go now, Natalie,' I said, 'into the cave. It's perfect. We'll get harnesses from the climbing shed, bags from the hiking shed, and torches and stuff. No one will miss us for ages; we'll be back with the treasure – or at least the answers – before they miss us. What do you think?'

I actually bounced on my heels like an over-excited puppy as I outlined my plan to Natalie. I didn't even consider that she might refuse – and she didn't. She stared into my eyes without flinching and said, 'Yes, let's do it. Let's do it now.'

The rain pelted us as we ran from the hall in the direction of the hiking shed, but like Star on the afternoon of the first storm, I relished it. We were drenched through in no time so the rain couldn't make us any wetter – bring it on, I thought. I might have stopped and opened my arms to the storm, mimicking Star's actions, but I was too driven to follow my plan to pause to enjoy the moment. Like a berserker with frenzied power but little control, I whooped with pleasure as we ran.

We grabbed bags in the hiking shed, stuffing in water and trail mix, compasses and whistles. I put my blood kit and injector pen in the bag too. Even in my frenzy I was still a diabetic, and I may have been feeling foolhardy, but I wasn't suicidal. We were panting from our run, and didn't talk. In moments we were finished with the hiking shed, and after exchanging an excited look, we left and ran shrieking across the camp towards the climbing wall. There was no need to be quiet or furtive – who would hear us over the rain and thunder, or see us in the murky gloom? It was like we were the only ones alive in the whole deserted camp – like we owned the world.

The climbing equipment was kept in a shed behind the climbing wall. We huddled together in the confined space and helped ourselves to harnesses and ropes and cams and other bits of equipment. We hadn't actually done any climbing that wasn't on the climbing wall yet, but we'd talked about the theory. I knew that the cam clips could hold a person's weight if they were wedged into a crack in a rock, and that the belay devices created friction on the ropes that would stop you from freefalling. I was ready for it. At least I thought I was.

Getting outside the camp boundary was a challenge. We searched up and down the new security fence, looking for a breach, but the wire was sound and our hearts started to fall. Surely we wouldn't be stopped by a fence!

Natalie had the idea to fold up the tarpaulin that covered the mat – the one that Mark had used as his magician's cloak – and lay it over the sharp wire that topped the fence. When the razor wire was safely covered, we threw our climbing equipment over, then I lifted Natalie on to my shoulders, and she slid across the tarpaulin and down the other side. Getting me over was harder. Natalie tried grabbing my wrists and hauling me up, but that was no good: I was too heavy and she had no leverage. Instead I had to search about for any pieces of equipment that weren't nailed down and build a tower of tyres and planks of wood that I was eventually able to climb up until I could jump down on the other side of the fence.

When we were both standing on the ground outside camp I started to feel fear for the first time. But I didn't want to go back. We'd crossed the line by breaking out of the camp boundaries and for better or for worse we were committed. Natalie didn't seem to be afraid. She looked radiant, like she'd lived for that moment. Her happy expression spurred me on, and I grinned at her, forgetting my fear.

'The entrance to the cave is over there,' I said. 'Matt and I saw it from up in the rope course. There's yellow tape around it.' It was only early afternoon, but the storm clouds effectively cut off most of the sun's light so that under the trees it was almost as dark as night-time.

I brushed away handfuls of leaves – sodden in the rain

that was heavy enough to filter through the canopy of trees above – and I saw the yellow tape. Ropes lay on the ground within the taped-off area, coiled and half-buried in the rotted leaf matter. They looked like they'd lain there undisturbed for some time, years even, except for a loop that had pulled away from the rest of the coil and lay on top of the fallen leaves. It must have been the loop of rope that had tripped up Star. It acted as an arrow pointing me in the right direction to find the opening, but even then it was difficult to spot it. I stared at the ground blindly for minutes until the crack jumped out at me like an optical illusion that is hidden until the moment of realisation, but which once you have spotted it seems obvious.

'Here,' I said, 'here's the entrance.'

The rope may have fed into the hole at one point – the end nearest the hole was frayed unevenly, as if it had been chewed or roughly worn away.

Natalie and I knelt at the edge of the hole and tried to peer into its depths, but it was like trying to look into an inkwell. I picked up a rock and threw it into the crack, and we heard it hitting the sides more times than we thought possible before eventually the noise stopped, so it must have reached the bottom.

Businesslike, we harnessed up, checking each other's clips as had been drilled into us by the climbing instructors.

'I'll go first,' I said, chivalrously.

I sat on the edge of the crack, my legs dangling down into it, and slid a cam clip into what looked like a reasonable crack at the top of the rocky side of the fissure. I gave it an experimental tug, and the metal top of the clip fanned out, wedging it in place.

For some reason, the thought of descending into the gloom of the cave entrance was for me ten times scarier than launching off from a great height. I started to feel panicky. My hands became clammy; my breath came out in short gasps.

'Are you all right?' Natalie asked. 'Do you want me to go first?'

'No, I'm fine,' I said, determined not to look stupid. The fear of embarrassment must have been greater than my fear of confinement, because I scooted my bum off the edge then, and lowered myself into the gap.

It was really dark. We didn't have helmets with lights attached like potholers or miners might use – if I'd have given the crazy mission more thought, I might have rigged up something like that, but I hadn't. I needed both my hands for climbing, so I turned on my torch and wedged it into the waistband of my jeans so that the light pointed upwards, which really didn't help when I looked down, but at least it stopped the feeling of being crushed by the complete darkness that had filled the hole before I turned it on. And at least it would light the way for Natalie.

It was just like abseiling, only slower, more controlled. A lot slower in my case because each time I allowed more rope to feed through my belay device I had to psych myself up and fight the urge to scramble back up to the glorious, spacious outside world. Natalie soon caught up with me, which made matters worse because not only was I hemmed in on all sides, but from above as well.

'Hurry up!' she said, more than once.

'I am hurrying,' I said, through teeth that I couldn't help gritting. 'I can't see my feet.'

'I would have gone first, you know,' she said. 'Hold on.'

I could hear fumbling above me, and then light shone down into my upturned eyes. I blinked to get rid of the green crescents that now obliterated my field of vision, and saw that the light did reach past me a little into the shadows below.

'I turned my torch upside down,' Natalie said.

'Thanks.'

I thought of my torch, wedged in the waistband of my jeans, and wondered how she'd managed to get hers to point down.

'How d'you do that?' I called up.

'What?'

'Why isn't the light just shining down the leg of your jeans?'

'It's not in my jeans,' she called back, and then after a second she added, 'It's in my bra.'

'Oh.'

I couldn't help imagining the torch in Natalie's bra, and in spite of my feelings of claustrophobia, I smiled.

'Cool.'

'Well, when you're finished imagining my bra, maybe we could start moving again?' she said.

How did she know?

I know it sounds dumb, or maybe a bit pervy, but I focused on the image of Natalie's bra as I forced myself to go deeper and deeper into the chimney. Even when the walls were touching my shoulders on both sides and I thought I would surely be stuck for ever with the weight of thousands of tons of rock slowly crushing me to death, I thought, 'Another step down – maybe it's white. Down some more – it might be pink. Move your leg – perhaps it has lacy bits. It's wider now – would I be able to work the clasp? YES!'

My legs splayed out wildly as the narrow vertical tunnel ended and I was suspended over an open cavern. Thanking the patron saint of lingerie, I lowered myself the last few feet and then collapsed on to the ground.

- Fifteen -
ECHOES IN THE DARK

I lay on the floor of the cave, so relieved to be out of the
narrow chimney that I felt elated. When Natalie landed,
moments after me, I pulled myself up on my elbows and
grinned at her. I caught a tiny glimpse of her bra as she
extricated the torch: it was yellow, or maybe it was
white – everything looked different in the torchlight. I
held my own torch up against my face to uplight it in an
eerie way and said, 'Welcome to my secret lair, little girl!
Mwa ha ha ha!'

She just smiled at me, and we lay there beside each
other for a while longer, until the cold and the hardness
of the rock forced us to move. We stood up and
removed the bulky climbing harnesses and ropes, letting
them drop in a pile on the ground beneath the ropes
that still hung down from the tunnel above.

There was a small pile of cigarette stubs on the ground.
They instantly made me think of Drew – he was the only
person I'd seen smoking at camp. Had Drew been down
into the cave? But why? Was it Drew who had beaten up
Star? But surely she would have told me if it was Drew

when I saw her in the infirmary – wouldn't that have been more important than showing me her clue? But she *was* desperately trying to tell me something when they were taking her away. Maybe she was trying to tell me about Drew then and there wasn't enough time?

By shining the torches into all the corners of the cavern, we could see that it was about the size of one of the sleeping cabins. Dark tunnels led off in three different directions, as well as the one above us through which we'd entered.

It occurred to me that we hadn't really thought through what we would do once we were in the caves. Part of me wanted to climb straight back out again – but I thought, no, since we're here we should at least look around.

'What now?' I said. 'Which way should we go?' My voice sounded strangely echoey.

'We should look around this first cavern really thoroughly first,' Natalie said, 'in case there are any clues, or a map, or even the treasure itself.'

The area had looked pretty empty when we swept our torches about, but it made sense to check more thoroughly. After a few minutes, though, it was clear that there was nothing – nothing but the cigarette stubs, and some loose rocks and dust and something that I assumed was guano.

'How about we each take one of the three tunnels, and go down it about, I don't know, fifty paces, then come back and tell the other one what we saw?' Natalie said. 'Then we'll look at the third tunnel together.'

I didn't much like the idea of heading down one of the dark tunnels on my own, but before I could voice my concerns, Natalie said, 'I'll take this one,' and she climbed over a rock that obstructed the entrance to one of the tunnels and disappeared into the gloom. I chose the entrance that looked the least claustrophobic and tentatively stepped through it.

I walked slowly, counting my paces and looking for signs of anyone having been there before me. The tunnel was pretty straight with a steady decline taking me deeper under the ground. After fifty paces I hadn't seen anything interesting. The path continued as far as my torchlight could illuminate, but I turned and headed back to Natalie anyway.

She was waiting for me when I got to the cavern.

'My tunnel was a dead end,' she said. 'I only got about twenty paces in and then I had to come back.'

I told her that mine kept going and might be worth another look.

Natalie picked up a sharp rock and scratched it against the wall of the cave. It left a thin, pale line, just visible when she shone her torch on it. 'Look,' she said, 'we can mark the two entrances with these rocks, like chalk. I'll put an X by mine, and a tick by yours, in case we forget which is which.'

It seemed like a good idea. After Natalie marked the tunnels, we headed together down the third, unexplored tunnel.

This tunnel started off pretty narrow, and got narrower still as we went on. Walking along it wasn't quite as bad for me as lowering myself into the vertical shaft, but it wasn't far off it. It doesn't really make sense that I would feel safe in the cavern, but not safe in a narrow tunnel – I mean, the ceiling of the cavern could just as easily fall as the ceiling of a tunnel, couldn't it? It was just the sense of being trapped or confined in the tunnels that I didn't like. Combined with the sense of the unknown, I guess. Once or twice we had to push through a constriction and I breathed sighs of relief when the tunnel widened again. I hated the feeling of not being able to move my limbs as we squeezed through the gaps – and my biggest fear was being trapped that way for ever.

Natalie didn't seem to be bothered by the narrow passageways. In fact, she looked happier than I'd seen her all summer. She was even humming. The sound of her voice echoed up and down the tunnel, until it sounded like it was coming from all around us. Our footsteps echoed too; it sounded like we were being followed, which spooked me, but I made myself calm down, told myself it was simple physics – sound bouncing off hard walls, that's all. Or was it?

'Natalie, shhh!' I said suddenly, turning to face her with my finger to my lips.

'What?'

'Do you hear that?'

The steps continued after we stopped. Just for a moment – tap tap – then silence. Too long to be just our echoes.

Someone was in the caves with us.

'What? How's that . . . I mean, who is that?' Natalie

looked confused and, for the first time since we came over the fence, worried.

'Do you think it's, you know, the clue-sender?' I said, keeping my voice quiet so that whoever it was wouldn't hear me, even though I knew it was probably futile considering how much sound travelled in the caves.

'No!' she said. 'I don't know. Why would someone be down here?' She didn't sound so much frightened as angry. I shone my torch into her face and she brushed her hand through the beam as if it was a troublesome insect that she could swat away.

Natalie may not have been frightened, but I was. We didn't even know if the tunnel we were in led anywhere. We could have been walking into a dead end with our only way out being the way we came in – the way that someone else was coming now.

'Whoever it is is probably still a long way behind us,' Natalie said. 'That sound was pretty quiet. If we keep moving we'll still have time.'

'Yeah,' I said. 'Have time for what?' I asked her.

In the dim light from her downward-pointing torch she looked thoughtful. Then with a shrug she said, 'To find the treasure. That's all. Isn't that what we're here for?'

'Yeah.'

When she put it like that, for a moment I forgot to be afraid. I was Indiana Jones searching the pharaoh's tomb for treasures. With just a flick of my whip I could disarm the bad guys and hook the golden idol in one swift move. The soundtrack played in my head – der de der dum, dum de dooo. I could run from rolling boulders and leap gaping chasms, and all with a rakish smile at the ladies. Oh yeah.

Just then something flew past my head and I screamed like a girl.

'Shh!' said Natalie. 'It was a bat. Just a bat. It's all right.'

My heart was pounding and I was hot with embarrassment. So much for being the hero. More like the cowardly sidekick who's added to the story for comedy value. The echoes from my scream seemed to take ages to die away, and as they did, my fear returned. There's no way our pursuer could not have heard that. I might as well have shouted, 'Here I am. Come and get me!'

'Come on,' said Natalie. 'We need to hurry up.'

We kept checking the walls and floor for anything that might give us a clue, but we saw nothing.

At last the tunnel widened. Twice there were forks, and Natalie scratched the way we took with her rock to mark our route. It occurred to me that whoever was following us only had to look for the mark to see which way we'd gone.

'Make a small mark, low down,' I told her at the second fork. 'So it's not obvious unless you know where to look.'

'Yeah. Good idea,' she said.

After we'd been walking a long time, there was a third fork. We took the right tunnel, marking the wall with the rock. We stood still for a moment and listened. Silence. Could we have lost our pursuer?

Shortly afterwards the wall receded smoothly, effectively making a little nook that we could sit in.

'Let's take a break,' I said. I was tired and my feet hurt. We sat on our backpacks, after taking out water and some trail mix to eat. We laid our torches on the ground, and I saw that mine was noticeably less bright than Natalie's. It was flickering too.

'Maybe I should turn my torch off,' I said. 'It looks like the battery is dying.'

'Yeah,' Natalie agreed. 'We should have just used one all the time. To save batteries. I wasn't thinking.'

Not thinking. Now that I look back my mind is screaming out at me: what was *I* thinking! How did I ever think it was a good idea to wander around in underground tunnels after mythical treasure?

As we sat there I suppose I *was* starting to regret my rash actions. In my head I was going over what might happen next. If we did find treasure – then what? If it was big, we would never be able to carry it out of the tunnel. And if it was small then why were we wasting our time with it anyway? I was so deep in thought that I jumped when Natalie started talking.

'What did you say?' I asked her. 'Sorry, I was miles away.'

'I said,' she repeated, 'my real dad committed suicide.'

I suppose I should have been used to Natalie's habit of saying things completely out of the blue like that, but still I was quite taken aback. I was glad of the dark because my gaping expression probably looked more stunned than sympathetic.

'Wow,' I said. 'How did he . . . I mean, why did he . . . um, how did you find out?'

'He hanged himself,' she snapped, her voice accusatory, as if it was *my* fault that her dad was dead, 'when I was two years old. He killed himself because of my stepdad.'

(Not my fault then, but she did blame somebody.)

'I found out when I was nine.'

I didn't say anything. What could I say? Natalie went on anyway:

'Do you remember when we did that thing for Mr Kenyan, about researching our family trees?'

'Yeah, I remember.' Mr Kenyan had taken his special class on a trip to the library to look up our family trees. We'd filled the details of our ancestors into photocopied tree pictures – it was pretty cool, I still had mine hanging on my bedroom wall.

'I searched in the newspaper archives for my stepdad's name, Alexander Anderson – except at the time I thought he was my dad, not my stepdad,' Natalie said.

'I found a news story:

LOCAL LOVE-TRIANGLE MAN TAKES HIS OWN LIFE

'It said that my dad – his name was David, David Carter – it said that he and my mum and my stepdad had been best friends since they were little kids. It said that they did everything together, but then that my mum and dad fell in love and got married and had me. But behind my dad's back, his best friend, my stepdad, was doing it with my mum. He walked in on them one day. Having sex. He'd come home from work early – they weren't expecting him. The paper put it in some sick sensationalist way – like, "he surprised them as they lay entwined in their secret lovers' embrace".'

Her voice caught as she said it, and she took a few shuddering breaths before going on.

'He walked out, and went back to his office, where he worked. He stayed there until everyone else had gone home for the night, and then he hanged himself. They found him in the morning. Dead.'

I sat in the dark silence listening to her story. My mum hadn't told me the whole truth, then, when I'd asked her about Natalie's stepdad. I guess she thought I was too young to hear something like that. And yet Natalie had heard it – or read it. How horrible for her. She'd been only nine years old.

'Can you believe my mum married him then?' she said. 'And they didn't even tell me. They let me believe that that murderer was my dad.'

'But,' I said without thinking, 'he didn't murder your dad – your dad killed himself.'

'HE KILLED HIM!' she shouted, making me jump. 'As surely as if he'd stabbed him through the heart with a dagger. Can't you see that? And then they went on playing happy families as if everything was all right. As if they deserved to be happy. They even showed me photos of when they were together as kids. They told me that the boy with them was just an old friend who they'd lost touch with. They lied to me.

'But I got my revenge.'

178

The way she said that last sentence made my blood run cold. What did she mean, she got her revenge? Her mum and stepdad were dead. Was Natalie saying that she was glad they had an accident? That she was glad that they died?

'What . . .' My voice was croaky, so I cleared my throat and tried again. 'What do you mean?'

'I spent weeks planning it,' she said calmly, 'months even. Do you remember our tenth birthday party – we had it in your back garden? I got your mum to give me the cardboard tube that the roll of paper tablecloth stuff came on – that was for making the flares. Even then I was getting things ready.'

I felt uncomfortable. What was Natalie telling me? What had she been planning? Why was she making cardboard flares? A horrible suspicion began to rise in me, but I wouldn't let myself even form it into words in my mind. It couldn't be true, could it?

'Everything had to be perfect,' she said. 'The engine had to work long enough for him to get way out to sea, too far to be seen from the land. The radio too – if it had been broken before he set off, he might have postponed the trip until he got it fixed. In the end, for the radio I just put in a fuse that was too few amps, so it would burn out when the battery powered by the boat's engine surged. And in the engine I weakened some of the moving parts so they would break when they got too warm. Pretty clever I thought – for a ten-year-old.'

Memories flooded my mind: Natalie learning how her stepdad's boat radio worked, Natalie taking apart the boat engine. Natalie's mum and stepdad going sailing and never coming back. There was no record of them radioing a distress signal, no one spotted any flares. They just vanished. It was almost as if someone staged the accident.

'Natalie,' I said, willing her to laugh it off and give me a different explanation, 'did you kill your parents?'

She ignored the question, as if it was irrelevant, and continued with her monologue.

'Of course I had to take his signal flares too. I replaced them with the fakes I made out of the cardboard tube – like something out of *Blue Peter*. He would have spotted they were fake if he'd picked them up and really looked at them, but I figured he probably wouldn't check them at all, and if he did it would just be a quick glance.

'I drilled holes in the bottom of his boat. Do you remember the hand drills we had in woodwork? I took one of those. They weren't very powerful, but with patience they could get through the hull of a boat. They were quiet too. No noisy whirring to arouse suspicion.

'Just tiny holes, so it would take a long time for the boat to sink.

'Everything was perfect.

'Except for one thing.'

I listened with horrified fascination. It was like a radio play – her voice in the darkness. Like it wasn't real. But it was real. There was no way she was making this up.

'What thing?' I said. 'What went wrong?'

'MY MUM WASN'T SUPPOSED TO BE THERE!'

BE THERE ... BE THERE ... BE THERE ...

I wasn't sure if the echoes were real or in my mind.

Then Natalie made a sound like an animal in pain. A primitive wail of sadness.

'I didn't want to kill my mum.' Her voice was quiet now, tiny, but in the stillness I could hear her anyway. 'She wasn't supposed to be there. It wasn't her fault. It was his fault. Men only have one thing on their minds. All men. They're pigs! I wanted me and my mum to be together. Just the two of us. It's not fair. Why did she go with him?'

Natalie began to sob quietly but I didn't move towards her or try to comfort her. I didn't move at all as I took in what she'd said. She'd murdered her parents. Not even in a flash of fury that she regretted. She planned it in cold blood. I didn't feel pity for her. I felt revulsion.

So she was only nine or ten years old. *So* she'd had a terrible shock. That didn't make it all right. I had played with her, and thought it was cool that she understood engines, never suspecting that she was planning a murder.

I felt sick.

- sixteen -
TOGETHER TILL WE DIE

We turned off both torches then. It seemed like a good idea to preserve the batteries, plus I thought that who-ever it was whose footsteps we'd heard following us in the cave would probably have a torch of their own, so if we were in the dark then we would have the advantage of being able to see them coming.

I didn't feel much like going on, but then I didn't feel much like staying either, and going back wasn't an option – at least not until we knew who was following us and why.

We sat in silence for a while, and I was just about to turn on my torch and suggest we get going when Natalie started speaking again.

'When I saw you in the airport in London,' she said, 'I was so happy. I couldn't believe it was you. I thought there was no way fate would send me something good for a change. And then I thought maybe it was fate, or God, or something – my second chance. I thought you would be my saviour. I thought finally I would be happy again. I thought I could trust you, that you would care for me.

'When you and me were kids, playing together,' she said, 'that was – well, it was the happiest time in my life. When we lay side by side on the floor in my bedroom working out codes. Do you remember? You were the only person who I felt ever *got* me. Like we were the same. Like we were meant to be together. Kindred spirits, you know?'

She paused, expecting me to agree, I guess. And I did agree. We *were* kindred spirits back then, but not any more, not now, so I said nothing. She didn't press me for an answer – maybe she thought I had nodded in the darkness. She went on:

'I just wanted things to be like they were. You and me together again, solving clues, being the good guys. And it would have worked too, if it wasn't for her.'

I still didn't get it. It was like my supposedly genius mind was stuffed with cotton wool. Her words didn't make any sense to me.

'I knew you would bring the first clue to me, but still my heart leapt when you did,' she said, and finally in my mind, the penny began to drop.

'You . . . ?' I spluttered. 'You made the clues?'

'Yes, I made the clues.'

'But . . . what about the treasure?' I said, not under-standing what was going on. 'Why are we here? And who . . . who's following us?'

'There would have been treasure,' she said. 'The best gift a girl can give a boy. It's what you all want, isn't it? It would have been good. But you messed up. You went after any girl who would look at you. You went after Star.'

I thought of Star being lifted away bruised and in agony. I thought of her saying someone might had grabbed her ankle before she fell. The shaft we'd climbed down to get into the caves was twisted and rocky with a long drop at the bottom. I could see how falling down it would have injured Star badly.

'If you sent the clues, then you must have put the clue under Star's pillow . . .' I said. 'You were luring her out here so you could push her into a cave. You . . . you could have killed her! She could have died!'

'Star? Yeah.' Natalie's voice sounded light, amused even. 'Who knew she'd be so bouncy?'

'You're mad!' I said, still not believing what was happening. This was Natalie. My childhood friend, my clue-solving buddy, casually confessing to attempted murder.

She ignored my comment and went on with her narrative.

'She was a bad influence on you. At least I thought so. Because my Luke isn't like other men, I thought. But I was wrong, wasn't I, Luke? You're just like other men. You don't think about other people's feelings, do you? You don't care who loves you, who would live or die for you, do you? You just want to have a good time. To notch up your conquests so you can brag about them to your mates later.

'I THOUGHT YOU WERE DIFFERENT!' she screamed madly, and I recoiled from the sound.

'I'm not a man, though,' I said, my voice sounding shaky and almost tearful. 'I'm fifteen. I'm just a boy. Life

184

should be fun, not serious. We're too young to think about love.' I was making excuses to myself as much as her because what she said had made me feel guilty. I guess I do kind of think of girls in terms of their bits, rather than their feelings. But what I said was true too. I'm a teenager, not an adult. I wasn't about to settle down and start a family or anything like that. What did she expect?

'Oh poor little boy Luke,' she said sarcastically. 'What a pity you never got to grow up. Life isn't about fun and fairy tales. Mark was right when he told you that life isn't nice. Life isn't nice, and people aren't nice, and you can't trust anyone.'

'No,' I said. Maybe I shouldn't have tried to argue with Natalie, considering I'd just found out she was willing to kill people she didn't like, but I still couldn't accept that the world was as bad as she said. 'Lots of things in the world are nice – my family ...' (Except for Ryan, I thought, but didn't say out loud – and even he was maybe not so bad, considering he has to put up with me getting all the attention because I'm younger and because I'm diabetic.) 'Ashley is nice ...'

'Oh yeah,' Natalie spat, 'she's nice because you thought you were going to get somewhere with her. Don't tell me you were interested in her for her conversation?'

'Actually,' I said, rising to the bait, 'we have a lot in common. If she hadn't had got sick ...'

'Ha!' Natalie laughed. 'That was precious. It couldn't have worked out better. You came over at just the right moment. Predictable as ever. When Arleen told us which mushrooms induced vomiting, I had no idea they would produce such spectacular vomiting. I wish I'd had a camera.'

'You? You fed her poison mushrooms?'

I suppose I shouldn't have been shocked by anything Natalie did any more, but still I was.

'Well, duh,' she said. 'Did you not think it was very convenient that so many people suddenly got sick? Did you think it was just a coincidence that only you and I were left to look for the "treasure"? Come on, Luke, I thought you were smart. I thought you might have worked that one out. But then, you didn't get the glaringly obvious clue in the talent show, did you?'

'What clue?' I said. 'What are you talking about?'

'Oh, Luke, you're making this too easy for me,' she said, sighing. 'The poem?'

I remembered the poem. Of course I did – with my near-photographic memory I could see it on the page written out as she gave it to me.

I stared at it in my mind for several seconds until I saw what she meant.

'It's acrostic.'

Intelligence pays,
At least this year it has done,
My smarter than average buddies.
The reward – well, we're here,
Having fun in the sun,
Even hiking through fields that are muddy!

Camp life, how we love you, from
Leathercraft to climbing, to sleeping out
Under the stars (howwwlll!)
Every creature that lives here's my
Sister and Brother
(Except mozzies and coyotes and bears).
Now listen, you guys who I've come to admire,
Dear friends I don't want to forget,
Everybody come closer, and listen to me,
Ready? Good, now you're going to get wet!

The first letter of each line together spelled out the message '**I AM THE CLUE SENDER**'. An acrostic poem – one of the most ancient types of code. And I'd missed it.

The tunnel echoed with Natalie's slow claps. 'Oh well done,' she said. 'You got there in the end.'

So Natalie sent the clues. Natalie got Star out of the way. She poisoned Ashley, and Matt and lots of other people too. And now I was down a cave with her, in the dark. What was she planning to do to me?

That's when I realised that I had to get away from her. But without my torch I wouldn't be able to move very well. Even though we'd been sitting in the dark for some time, my eyes hadn't adjusted – at least, I still couldn't see anything at all. The caves could be treacherous and if I fell and hurt myself then I would be a sitting target for her. Trying not to make a sound, I reached out my hand and felt around for the torches.

'Aiee!' My fingers found not the torches, but warm

flesh. Natalie's hand was resting over my torch.

'What are you doing?' she asked, her voice tinged with suspicion.

'Nothing,' I said. 'Just stretching.'

'If you try to run away I'll find you,' she said. 'There's no escape, Luke.'

In my mind I was formulating a plan – all I had to do was retrace our steps, and then climb back out of the cave using the rope we'd left dangling. As if she was reading my mind, Natalie said:

'You can forget about climbing out. I've taken care of that.'

'What? What do you mean?'

I felt something cold touch my arm and I flinched. The movement was accompanied by a small but hot pain.

'Careful, Luke,' Natalie said. 'We don't want you getting hurt. Yet. Knives are dangerous, you know.'

Drew's knife. She'd taken Drew's knife.

'I cut the rope,' she said. 'When I said we should split up and explore the tunnels, that was just to get you out of the way – you're so trusting. Whatever happens now, we're both stuck down here.'

My desire to get away from Natalie intensified, but I had to play it cool. I needed a torch, or I'd have no hope of getting anywhere.

'If I don't run away,' I said, 'what will you do to me then?'

I didn't expect her to answer. Didn't want her to answer. I was just trying to distract her. Perhaps if I could get her talking, I thought, she would lift her hand off the torch and I could make a run for it.

She laughed. A flat, hollow laugh that literally sent shivers down my spine. 'I read up on the area before I came,' she said, in what seemed to be a non sequitur. 'I wanted to go out with style, you know. I thought jumping off a cliff would be cool – a cliff at the top of a mountain so I could run across the grass and then fly away off the edge like a bird. But down here will do. It's better, in fact – there's a certain poetic justice to being lost underground. Like my mum, lost at sea. I'm doing you a favour bringing you with me. You're too innocent, too naïve. Life in the real world would only break your heart. We were always meant to be together. Together till we die.' Her hand reached up and stroked my face, gently, almost tenderly.

If her hand is on my face, I thought, it isn't on the torch. I tried to keep my head absolutely still as my fingers walked across the floor looking for the unguarded flashlight.

'Besides,' she said, and her hand left my face, 'you don't deserve to live. Neither of us does. I'm a murderer, and you're a . . . HEY!'

I'd got it. As soon as the torch was in my grasp I jumped to my feet, grabbing the handle of my backpack and already starting to run.

No! Pressure from my bag jerked me back. She had hold of the straps, she was tugging and I'd lost the element of surprise. I had a split second to decide what to do, and in that split second the need to escape overruled the

189

part of my brain that was telling me I needed the bag – that I needed the water, and the food, and especially the insulin. The present danger of Natalie with a knife had to take precedence over the future danger of uncontrollable blood sugar, so I dropped the bag and ran.

'You need me!' Natalie shouted after me. 'We need each other. You'll come back.'

As I ran away, I banged my head against a jagged lump of rock that jutted out of the wall. I bit my lip so hard in an attempt not to cry out that blood trickled down from my mouth, as well as from above my right eye. Still I didn't want to turn on my torch until I was far enough away from her.

Running, running, running through the dark.

How long would it be until I couldn't run any more?

part two

The Cave

- seventeen -
LOST

And now I'm walking and trying to make sense of it all. I thought going through it from the beginning would help, but it hasn't. I still can't believe it. I still can't see the Natalie from my childhood, or the Natalie from the past few weeks as the same Natalie who I'm running from. The Natalie who killed her parents and now wants to kill me.

The missing campers (if they even existed) have nothing to do with this. The counsellors have nothing to do with this, since the clues came from Natalie. I didn't find trouble in America, I brought it with me.

Who will help me now? The others don't know the truth – they still probably think that Captain Bud or Drew are behind it all. They'll be afraid to go to them for help, just like we were afraid to go to them when Star was missing.

My hands, still slicked with blood, slip on the walls. It crosses my mind absurdly that I could use the blood from my injuries to test my glucose level. Pricking my thumb for the blood test still makes me wince worse than administering the insulin shots. But no, I've forgotten already – my testing kit is in my backpack, along with everything else I need to keep me alive. My backpack that Natalie has.

It's not that long since lunch, and I ate some trail mix when Natalie and I first sat down. Eating usually makes my blood glucose peak, and then I have to have some insulin to bring the level down again, but other things can bring down my blood sugar: like exercise, or anything that makes my heart beat faster or my metabolism race – like being lost in a dark labyrinth with someone who I thought was my oldest friend but who turned out to be my most deadly enemy. That would do it.

Could I guess my blood sugar without the testing kit? Do I know my body well enough to tell if I'm going hypo or hyper? I should be able to, but then my body is so pumped full of adrenalin right now that it's hard to concentrate on anything but the fear that threatens to overwhelm me. Besides, what difference would it make? With no food and no insulin, there would be nothing I could do anyway.

I try again to calm myself, both to regulate my metabolism and to lower the levels of adrenalin in my system. I want to work off the sugar in my system, but not so fast that the levels go dangerously low. My breaths are short and jerky and it takes all my concentration to control them, to make them slower. I remember that people say you should imagine a lovely place in your mind to cope with stress. A beach – isn't that what they say? Imagine that you're lying on a beautiful beach in the sun, with palm trees and seagulls. I close my eyes and picture the pale golden sand, the warm salty air and the sound of the sea caressing the shore in shades of translucent blue and green. It helps as well, at least a little. I don't feel quite so filled with panic.

When I open my eyes again I turn on the torch. I figure I'm far enough away from Natalie now for her not to see. The beam it produces is weak and yellow, but it still makes a huge difference in the total darkness of the cave.

I'm still walking, but I start to think that I should come up with a plan. To walk aimlessly could only get me more lost, more difficult to find.

I should retrace my steps, find the first cavern. There might be enough of the rope left for me to climb up. I could find one of the leaders, tell them everything. They could go down and get Natalie, and then everything would be all right again.

I'm turning around, shining my torch to light my way. I won't run – there's no point in running now and risking falling or using too much blood sugar. It's better to be safe than sorry.

As I walk, for some reason I sing nursery rhymes. Songs that have been buried in my memory for years from a time when life was as simple as scraped knees and mother's hugs and warm milk and bathtime.

'One, two, buckle my shoe. Three, four, knock at the door.'

My voice is thin and shaky, and yet the sound gives me some comfort. I surprise myself with the repertoire of remembered words that come from my mouth. It becomes a challenge – to move seamlessly from one song to the next without repeating myself. I run out of nursery rhymes, so I move on to songs from *The Wizard of Oz* – 'Follow the Yellow Brick Road', 'If I Only Had a Brain'. I almost feel jaunty, like I could kick my heels and skip down the dark tunnels.

> When a man's an empty kettle,
> He should be on his mettle –
> And yet I'm torn apart.
> Just because I'm presumin'
> That I could be kind of human –
> If I only had a heart.

Instead of finishing the Tin Man's song, I stop singing. I don't know if it is because the words have struck a chord. Wasn't that why Natalie was so angry at me, angry enough to want me dead – because I didn't consider other people's feelings, her feelings? Because I was heartless? Or maybe I've stopped because it has occurred to me that I've been singing for a long time and I haven't reached any of the forks in the path that Natalie and I passed on our way.

With this realisation, I feel a physical sensation like a cramping in my chest, like someone has suddenly grabbed my insides and squeezed.

I'm lost.

I'm under the ground thousands of miles from home and I'm lost.

Did I take a turning in the dark when I first ran from

Natalie? I must have. There haven't been any turnings since I switched on the torch. What should I do? I'm going over options in my head but none of them seem like a good idea. I could keep going, hope that the tunnel I'm in will lead somewhere – but what if it doesn't? Or what if where it leads to is a dead end, or a treacherous drop? Or I could turn around, retrace my steps until I recognise where I am, then head back to Natalie, so she could say, I told you so, I told you you would come back.

What other options do I have, though? Staying still? How long would it take before I needed water, or food, or insulin? What would kill me first? Thirst or hypoglycaemia? Would they ever find my body? Would my parents mourn me? Would Ryan? Maybe Ryan would be happier if I died, then he'd be the only one getting my parents' attention. But no, I can't believe he would want me dead. We get along all right. As brothers go. I'll be more understanding if I survive, I'll be a better person, I'll appreciate him more. I'll appreciate everything more, if I get out. I don't want to die. Natalie was wrong to say life wasn't worth living. My life is worth living.

I want to live.

So staying still is not an option. The choice then is whether to go on, or to go back.

If I go on, the best thing that could happen would be finding a way out to the surface. The worst thing would be getting hopelessly lost, or trapped, or falling down a hole or something.

If I go back, the best thing would be that Natalie

would be gone, and I'd get to the first cavern and up the rope to freedom. Or maybe Natalie will still be there, but she'll have got over whatever it was that was making her act like a mad murderer and she'll say something like, oh Luke, you believed me, silly – it was all a joke, of course I wouldn't kill anyone. And then we'll go out of the cave together.

Or maybe she'll still be there and she won't have got over her madness. She'll be waiting for me with her knife. Would she really use the knife on me? If she's telling the truth and she engineered her parents' accident, as well as pushing Star into the cave, then she's not above causing the death of another person, but to stab someone with a knife – would she do that? It would be a violent and bloody act – did she hate me that much? I had to think that she would at least hesitate before plunging a knife into me. If I was prepared, maybe I could use her hesitation against her. Maybe I could grab the knife off her. I'm taller and heavier than her – the odds must be in my favour. I don't relish the thought of wrestling with Natalie over a knife, but I think it's a better idea than getting even more lost in the dark labyrinth of caves.

Yeah.

I've decided.

I have to go back.

Now that I've decided on a plan I move more quickly, eager to get the whole thing over with. I start to recognise little things that I'd noticed on the way: a strange stalactite that looked like a face peering down from the ceiling, that cleft in the rock that I'd thought at first was the entrance to another tunnel. After a while, though, I stop recognising things. The tunnel I'm in now looks unfamiliar, and I wonder if this was where I was when I was first running from Natalie, when the torch was turned off. I try to picture what the tunnel would be like just from the impression I got from my hands and my feet, but I can't. I keep walking anyway – every few steps I stop to see if I can hear anything. I wonder what is above me right now? Have I walked miles away from where I started already, or do the caves criss-cross beneath the camp? If I could bore a hole through the earth and rock above me, would I pop up like a mole in the riding stables? I wish that was the case. I wish I could look up and see curious faces of campers looking down on me. Where's Matt when I need him? Even a sarcastic comment from Drew would be welcome. 'What ya doing down there, boy? Did you think your lucky bear tooth could save you from being crushed by rocks?'

It's hard to keep track of time, but it seems to me that I should have got back to Natalie by now. I seem to have been walking for ages. I don't know if I would recognise the place where we sat and rested anyway – the place where I left her. I could have passed it; she could have gone somewhere else.

Yes, that's it, I'm thinking, Natalie's gone. I'm safe. All I have to do is keep walking until I come to the cavern, and then I'm out of there.

The happy feeling lasts for the next half-hour or so

before I start to realise that I really don't recognise anything. I know for a fact that Natalie and I had passed a fork not that long before we took a rest, but the tunnel I'm in just goes on and on. It's hopeless. I'm never getting out.

'HELP!' I scream, knowing it's futile, but doing it anyway. 'HELP! HELP! HELP!'

- Eighteen -
THE EVIL GENIUS

'HERE!'

Is it an echo? Did my shout of 'help' bounce back sounding like 'here'?

'LUKE? IS THAT YOU, LUKE?'

It's not an echo. Someone is calling me. A boy. A boy's voice is calling me.

'WHO IS IT?' I yell. 'WHERE ARE YOU?'

'IT'S ME – MARK.'

Evil Mark?

'I'M STUCK. HELP ME. PLEASE.'

Now I remember what I'd forgotten since running away from Natalie – that someone was following us when we were walking down the first tunnel. I said to Natalie that it must be the clue-sender, and she said no. She was confused. No wonder she was confused, since *she* was the clue-sender and she'd planned the whole going down into the caves thing and only she and I were invited. But Mark had followed us. He and Eoin had overheard about the treasure chest, about the 'quite beneath me' clue. And he'd decided to come and find the treasure for himself.

I'm torn between anger at him for making such a show of not believing in the treasure, when clearly he did, and relief that I'm not alone any more, even if the company is just about the last I'd have chosen.

'MARK, WHERE ARE YOU?'

'HERE.'

'KEEP SHOUTING. I'LL FOLLOW YOUR VOICE.'

I try to walk in the direction the voice is coming from, but when he calls again his voice is softer. I must be going the wrong way. I change direction, not quite believing I'm right – but sure enough, this time when I hear Mark shouting it's louder again.

'I'M COMING,' I call.

'HURRY!' he answers.

Our calls bounce back and forth between us, until I find the source of the sound – an opening at the side of the path. I walk through and find myself standing somewhere vast and echoey. I swing my torch around, taking in a cavern which is much larger than the one Natalie and I lowered ourselves into when we first entered the caves. There is a gorge or crack in the middle of the floor of the cavern that stretches right across it. The beam of torchlight is quickly swallowed by the shadows in the gorge, so there is no way for me to tell how deep it is.

Beyond the gorge, standing flat against the wall, with his arms splayed and feet balanced on a narrow ledge is Mark. As the light, pale though it is, finds his face he looks like a startled rabbit in headlights. Without the arrogant sneer that is his almost ever-present expression, he is barely recognisable. His face is dirty and smeared with tear-washed furrows. Like me he has bloody gashes on his forehead and arms. He has no torch or bag, although he does have a length of rope, coiled and slung over his shoulder.

It strikes me as strange, even funny (although I don't feel any urge to laugh), that from the moment I met Mark, I labelled him as the evil genius, and it turns out that it was Natalie all along who actually fulfilled that role. Not that that made Mark a saint or anything, but as I stand looking at him I see that he is just a boy, like me. He is scared and tired, and even though he's teased me and threatened me, when it comes down to it I know I have to help him. We have to help each other.

The beam of light dips from his face down to his feet, and I realise that I am losing my grip on the torch. I clench my hand, bringing the light back up, and feel my fingers shaking with the effort.

Numbness, tingling, shaking – the first signs of hypoglycaemia. My blood level is dipping. It's still slight. I don't feel dizzy yet. Normally a sweet or a drink of juice would be enough to sort me out if I feel like that. I don't have any sweets or juice, but I'll be all right for a while longer.

'How did you get there?' I ask Mark. 'Can you get over here?'

'I don't know.'

Mark's voice sounds different too – younger, less intimidating. I suppose I could gloat, enjoy seeing this boy who has acted so cockily towards me in such a state of weakness and vulnerability. And maybe I would have, even hours before. But somehow, after everything that has happened, after everything Natalie has said to me, I just don't feel like gloating.

'With your rope,' I say, 'one of us could get across.'

He doesn't answer, just looks at me.

'I don't know the way out from here,' I say. 'Do you remember what way you've come?'

'I'm stuck. I can't move.'

I sense that I am going to have to tread carefully. I speak gently to the boy who terrified me with his snarling lips and anger just days before. 'It's all right. I can help you. If you throw me the end of the rope we could make a sort of bridge, yeah? What do you think?'

Mark's fingers go to his shoulder, as if he is checking that he really does have a rope and that I'm not trying to trick him.

'A bridge?'

'Yeah.'

I look around to see if there is anything to tie the rope to. On my side of the gorge there is a rock sticking out of the ground that might do as an anchor. Mark's side looks less hopeful. He is standing on a narrow ledge and the wall behind him looks pretty smooth. I'm not sure that I want to trust Mark to hold the rope. I sink to the ground and sit with my arms wrapped around my legs, wondering what to do. I feel tired and irritable. Why should I have to save the day?

I turn out the torch for a while, to save the batteries.

Mark cries out when I do, 'No, please. Turn it on.'

He doesn't have a torch on him. He'd been in the dark when I found him. 'Why didn't you bring a torch?' I ask him.

'I did,' he says. 'I dropped it. It broke.'

Great.

'My batteries are running out,' I say. 'We should save them.'

'When we're both together on the same side,' he says. 'Then we can turn it off.'

Okay, I think, fair enough. I turn the torch back on.

'Throw me one end of the rope,' I say.

He pulls the coiled rope down his arm and holds one end while flicking the loops over like a frisbee. Thankfully the coils unravel beautifully as the rope flies across the gorge and lands to my left. I grab it quickly, since it has already begun to slide backwards, pulled by the slack middle which is dipping into the chasm. I wrap it twice around the rock, and try to remember the knots I was taught on the day that Star went missing. There was one for tying around logs, the 'timber hitch'. It was secure when pulled tight, but came loose when it went slack. If I could remember how to do it, then I could get across to Mark's side and then pull the rope after me. Since there is nothing to tie it to on Mark's side I can't see how to get him over to where I am. I don't much like the look of the narrow ledge on Mark's side, but at least we'd be together, and we're just as likely to find our way out on one side as the other, seeing I am totally lost anyway.

'Okay,' I mutter aloud to myself as I tie the knot. 'Around the rock, wrap the end over, and through, and twist, and twist again. That's it.'

'Pull it tight,' I say to Mark. He tugs and the rope goes taut. 'I need you to hold it,' I say. 'I'm going to have to climb over to your side, but you need to hold the rope tight or the knot will undo and I'll fall.'

This is the boy who's made my life a misery for the past few weeks with threats and put-downs. But I don't have any option but to trust him – to trust my life to him.

'Okay,' he says, bracing himself against the wall and looking like someone who is holding tight.

I ease myself over to the edge of the gorge, and lie back, wrapping my legs up and around the rope, and holding on with my hands, so I can crawl upside down across the gap. The rope sags worryingly as it takes my weight, and Mark shuffles his feet and wraps his end around his wrists. I edge on. The gap isn't big. I should be over in no time. Keep going Luke, you can do it. Good. That's it. I'm right in the middle now, too far to reach either the beginning or the end, and suddenly my blood turns to ice. I can hear a voice. Natalie's voice.

'Hello, boys,' she says.

Mark gasps in surprise and the distraction is enough to make him relax his hold on the rope just for a moment. The rope grabs its chance as if it's alive and snakes through his fingers, making him cry out as the friction burns his hands. I feel a moment of freefall, before the rope catches me and I swing painfully back

206

and down, banging into the wall of the gorge. I will my hands to hold on to the rope, but they stubbornly ignore me and let it escape from me too. Expecting to drop to my death, I am surprised to be caught short with a jolt moments after letting go of the rope. I lie winded on a ledge, and light from the torch which once again I'd wedged into the waistband of my jeans glints off something on the rocky ground beside me.

Bones.

Bones lie beside me. Actually complete skeletons, still wearing rags of clothes like macabre puppets. The Camp Hope logo is just visible on one of the T-shirts.

It's the missing campers.

Two of the skeletons have the fingers of their hands entwined, with more cigarette butts on the floor beneath them, while the third is missing the bottom half of its leg. I look around and see it, with the foot still attached, a little way away. The bone is broken jaggedly. I start to put together a story behind the remains.

The three missing campers went down into the caves. Who knows why? Not because of the clues, since Natalie was responsible for them. Maybe it was a dare, maybe an accident. It must have been them who left cigarette butts in the first cavern. One of them might have fallen and the others gone to rescue them. But no, then they'd have gone for help. It must have been a dare – an adventure at least. But they'd got lost; maybe their torches died and they couldn't see where they were going. They fell down the gorge. One broke his leg, the others stayed with their injured friend, waiting for help to come. But help had never come. They died and their memories were, well, not forgotten, but denied.

As I sit beside them I wonder if I am destined to join their party. Am I effectively one of the skeletons already, just not as decayed as the others? That's what Natalie wanted.

'Natalie. It's you. You scared me,' Mark is saying. I turn off my torch, hoping Natalie hasn't already looked down and seen me.

'Mark Blackwell. So you're the mysterious person who followed us down here,' she says. 'Okay. The more the merrier. I suppose Luke's told you about my evil plan?'

Although I can hear their voices, I can't see their faces or expressions. I imagine Mark's face changing from an expression of relief to confusion, maybe even fear.

'What do you mean? What evil plan?' He is laughing as he says it, but I can catch the edge of uncertainty in his voice.

'He hasn't told you?'

'Told me what?'

'Oh Luke!' Natalie raises her voice in a sing-song, lilted shout. 'Why didn't you tell Mark all about it? That's not fair, is it, keeping him in the dark like that? I don't think Mark likes being in the dark, do you, Mark?'

She lowers her voice, although I can still hear her.

'Did you know he calls you the Evil Genius, Mark?' she says, laughing. 'I thought you might get a kick out of that.'

She laughs some more, but I don't hear Mark laughing. Then there is a listening silence. I don't make a sound. If she thinks I am dead, maybe she'll go away.

'Luke!' she calls again. 'Where are you? Don't tell me you've died already without letting me watch.'

She turns her attention back to Mark.

'I came to camp to kill myself, you see, Mark,' she says. 'You were right when you said there were no nice people in the world. I'm not nice. My stepdad wasn't nice. My uncle certainly wasn't nice – wanting me to do things . . .' She pauses, and I remember her telling me that day when we were fishing that things hadn't worked out with her aunt and uncle. In my innocence it had never occurred to me that her uncle might have abused her. I was starting to understand why Natalie was so mixed up.

'He had an unfortunate accident,' she says, not sounding in the least bit sorry. 'Fell off a balcony. He didn't die, more's the pity – but let's just say he'll be easier to run away from now.

'Why would anyone want to live in a world with people like me in it?' she says, in a sing-song voice as if she is talking to little children or idiots. 'You should know what I mean, Mark. You're not as idealistic as the others. As Luke. Even Ashley, with her "Isn't everything beautiful and wonderful, and I love my life". She makes me sick. Don't you agree, Mark?'

'No.'

No? What? Listening from my perch below I do a double take. Is Mr Mean and Cynical Mark disagreeing with Natalie's bleak outlook?

Natalie's next words echo my own thoughts. 'What?'

'Luke's right,' Mark says quietly, 'and Ashley. It's us

209

that are in the dark. You and me. Not them. If they make me mad it's because they can do what I can't. They can be happy.

'So, my dad knocks me around. So, your uncle messed with you. That makes them bad, yeah, but not the whole world. Not us. At least it doesn't have to.'

I can't believe my ears. Evil Mark being wise and, well, nice.

Natalie is wrong-footed as well.

'But,' she splutters, 'it's not that simple. It's . . .'

'You're right,' Mark says. 'It's not simple. It's complicated and difficult, but it's worth working out. Maybe your uncle deserved what happened to him. But that's over now. You don't have to be the bad guy any more. You can start again. You can be normal. You're only, what, fifteen, sixteen? There's still time to turn your back on the bad things and start again.'

Wow. Mark sounds like a therapist. It occurs to me that he is maybe repeating what therapists have said to him. It doesn't matter where he got the words from, though, if they are winning Natalie around.

'You don't understand,' she says, but I think her voice holds a tiny spark of hope. 'You don't know me. You don't know what I've done.'

'Let it go,' he says. 'Move on.'

'I . . . I can't . . . I don't know . . .'

'You can.'

'I want to.' Her voice is small when she says that, and without the madly hysterical edge that has tainted it since she arrived in the cavern.

If I look up from my ledge I can see Natalie's torch making shaky sweeps around the cavern, sometimes pointing at Mark, sometimes swinging around as if she is gesticulating with her hands while she talks. I can see the ends of her feet hanging over the edge as she stands perilously close to the chasm in the ground. When she first started talking, she didn't seem to notice any danger, like she didn't care if she fell, but as she listens to his words she starts to move less – at least, from what I can see the movement of the light from her torch gets less. Then she suddenly shines her torch down at her feet as if she is finally realising the instability of her position. I hear her gasp, and see her feet shuffle as she stumbles. Then several things happen at once, too quickly to even separate them. The light from her torch, which is now pointing down, must have glinted in my eyes because she is suddenly looking right at me. The shock of seeing me, surrounded as I am by skeletons, must be what makes drop her torch and lose what is left of her balance. She teeters on the edge for agonising seconds before the momentum takes her and her body comes crashing down towards me.

'LUKE!' she screams. 'HELP ME!'

Her torch hits me on the head, reopening the partly healed wound where I'd bashed my head earlier. I ignore the fresh blood now dripping down my face and hold out my arms, grabbing at Natalie as she falls past me.

Yes! I've got her. Her hands grab my wrists, and mine in turn clamp around hers. The weight of her falling body almost pulls me off my ledge and down after her, but I just manage to brace myself and stop us both from falling.

She is hanging down from my ledge, looking up at me with frightened eyes.

'Luke, I'm sorry,' she says, and she sounds once again like the little girl I once knew. 'I don't want to die any more.'

'I'll save you,' I say, but even as I say it, her hands are slipping out of my grasp. My fingers are shaking and sweating and I just can't hold on.

'NO!'

Like a film in slow motion I watch her fingers slipping away from mine until they aren't touching at all, like she is hanging in air. But she isn't hanging, she is falling.

She falls for what seems like a lifetime, and then there is a sickening thud and a sound like the cry you make when someone punches you in the stomach, forcing out all the air from your lungs – an involuntary 'humph'.

'NATALIE!' I scream. 'NATALIE!'

Silence.

My torch has been off since Natalie entered the cavern, but hers that fell is miraculously still lit. It's shining through the bones of the lost campers and making huge dinosaur shadows on the wall behind them. I grab it and point it down into the depths of the gorge.

Natalie is lying at the bottom in a twisted, unnatural position.

She isn't moving at all.

Someone is shouting, 'NO! NO! NO!' I choke as the words compete with a sob that's rising in my throat and realise that it is me shouting.

'No.'

'Luke? Are you all right?' Mark calls down to me after

the echoes of my screams have died away.

'Yeah,' I call back. 'I'm all right. There's a ledge, not too far down. It broke my fall.'

I try to stand, but my head feels woozy and my legs wobble dangerously. I sit back down beside the skeletons.

'The missing campers are here too,' I call up. 'Their bones, at least.'

I shine the torch up, and see Mark's face looking down. I turn the torch back on myself to show him the other occupants of the ledge.

'Whoa,' he says, 'another mystery solved.'

'Yeah.'

I notice the rope then. It must have come loose from the rock after I fell, and is now draped over the shoulders of one of the skeletons. I try to untangle it from its bony perch but find that my fingers don't grip it well enough, and my mind can't work out which way to tug it anyway. The coils of rope blur before my eyes and I feel more confused. I forget what it was I was trying to do. The ground starts to move under me. I wonder if it's an earthquake, or maybe I'm at sea in a boat, or riding a camel – a ship of the desert. I don't know where I am. There are skeletons here in the boat with me. They are talking to me. 'Keep trying, Luke,' they're saying. 'Try to stay awake.' They are the skeletons out of the *Funnybones* books. What are they doing here in the desert? Shouldn't they be in a dark, dark town, down a dark, dark street?

I want to giggle, because the skeletons are funny.

Something is moving in the darkness. I don't understand why it is so dark. Someone should turn the light on.

Mum's shaking me. Get off, Mum, I want to sleep some more.

Now something is being tied around my chest and tugging on me and making me move. I must be a puppet, like Pinocchio. Maybe I'm not good enough to be a real boy.

I'm being pulled along the ground, or is it the wall? I don't know. There's a noise. It sounds like birds screaming, vultures or maybe pterodactyls, circling around me. They scream for a long time. Now they are lifting me. I wonder if it will hurt to be torn apart by the talons of the great birds. I'm not really scared, though – more interested than scared, like I'm watching some other Luke being eaten by birds. One of the birds bites me, a sharp jab, but instead of eating me it starts to go away. All the birds are going away and my mind feels like it's swimming up from deep water and I'm so close to the surface now I can see the sunlight through the ripples. There are men, not birds, around me. They are attaching ropes to me, and a harness, and one of them is saying, 'The injection of glucagons is working – he's coming round.'

It's suddenly very bright in the cave. The rescue workers have big powerful torches and ropes that lead the way back to the outside world. I allow myself to be carried like a baby along the tunnels and then pulled up the chimneystack in the first cavern until strong arms waiting at the top lift me out. Outside, the rain has stopped and the darkness is now the dark of night, not the dark of the storm.

Part Three
The End

- Nineteen -
CLOSURE

It's two weeks since I was lifted from the cave and now I'm back home in England. They closed the camp – for this year at least. Everyone got sent home. They're going to thoroughly explore the caves, map them out, make sure no one else gets lost down there. I guess they'll make a hatch or something over the hole that Natalie and I climbed in through. Maybe if they make it all safe, they'll add potholing to the activities next year. I can just imagine kids naming it the Ghost Walk or something.

I've been trying not to think about it, about Natalie, since I got home, but my therapist (yeah, I'm seeing a therapist – I guess so that I don't develop post traumatic stress syndrome or something) said that it's better to work through the memories, to analyse what happened and understand it all so I can move on. A lot of it is a blur to me – the time when I was hypo, at least – but Mark filled me in later on what happened. And Matt and the others told us what we'd missed in camp while we were underground.

My memory is pretty clear from the point when we were lifted from the cave. Mark and I were both checked over, and dressings were put on our scrapes and cuts. I could tell that Captain Bud and the sheriff really wanted to ask us questions about what had happened, but the medical team told them to let us rest. They did ask about Natalie, though, about what happened to her.

'She fell,' Mark said, in answer to their question. 'It was an accident. She lost her balance and fell.'

'I tried to catch her,' I said. 'I grabbed her wrists, but I couldn't hold her. I'm sorry.'

'That's enough now,' one of the medics said. 'These boys need rest and medical attention. Questions can wait.'

I think they must have given us sedatives as well as painkillers that night because I slept soundly. In the morning I was disorientated, waking up in a crisp white hospital bed in the camp infirmary with Mark in a bed beside me. The nurse brought us glasses of juice, checked our pulses and my blood glucose and then left us alone. It was my birthday. Sixteen. It would have been Natalie's birthday too.

There was an awkward silence for a while, and then I broke it and said, 'Hey.'

'Hey,' Mark echoed.

I wanted to ask him so much – like what had happened after I went hypo, and how the rescue team found us, and whether the whole business with Natalie was real and she was really dead. It was difficult to put it into words, though, especially with Mark, who had been my enemy – now I wasn't sure what he was.

He started talking, so I didn't have to. He told me that I'd really freaked him out in the cave by going all delirious and talking to the skeletons.

He said he kept talking to me, to try to keep me awake, and that sometimes I would say something that sounded almost sensible, but most of the time I just talked gibberish. Flashes of what he said found snapshots in my memory, but other things didn't spark anything, so it could have been someone else's story he was telling. He said he saw that there was a ledge below where he was standing, inside the gorge opposite mine. He lowered himself down – it must have taken a lot of courage for him to let go and drop the couple of feet down in the dark. Then he had to get across to me. The gap between the two ledges was smaller than at the top of the gorge, but still a long jump. I don't know if I'd have made it, or even attempted it, but he did. He said his mind didn't stop to worry about it. He *had* been horribly afraid, but he had pushed past his fear by then and was just working on autopilot. Once he was on my ledge he got the rope and tied it around my chest, under my arms. The other end he tied around the belt of his jeans and then he climbed up the wall of the gorge and back to the floor of the cavern. I guess it was kind of like the climbing wall – looking for handholds, or little bumps in the rock where he could wedge his feet. Except that it was dark, and he had no safety harness and no one to help him if he fell.

When he got to the top he tied the rope once again around the rock that jutted out of the ground. He saw that Natalie had left her bag and mine on the ground. There was water and trail mix in the bags, and Drew's knife, as well as my blood kit and injector pen, but by then I was too far gone to eat anything, and Mark knew enough at least not to try and give me any insulin.

It was the whistles that saved the day in the end.

I can piece together Mark's story with what Matt told me later that day about what was happening up in the camp. He said that when the storm stopped people realised that Natalie and I were missing. It took them a little longer to miss Mark – Eoin was in the infirmary after contracting the 'stomach bug'. Someone went there to check that Natalie and I hadn't started puking and been put to bed as well, and seeing Eoin reminded them to look for Mark too. The guys from the Chipmunk cabin discussed what to do and eventually decided that someone had to be told about everything. They didn't want to go to Drew, or Captain Bud either, so in the end they went to Brandy, the nature studies instructor, and told her all about the treasure hunt and the clues, and how Natalie and I had talked about looking for the treasure under the rope course.

The search and rescue teams were called in again, and this time they knew where the entrance to the caves was. They had a machine that they used above ground – an ultrasound, like what they use to look at unborn babies. With the ultrasound they located our bodies, but the caves were so labyrinthine that they still might not have found us were it not for Mark blasting away on the two whistles.

Matt asked me about what had happened in the caves, naturally, but I found I couldn't tell him everything. I couldn't bring myself to talk about Natalie's madness to him, about what she did to her parents and what she was trying to do to me. I had to tell him that Natalie had sent the clues, though.

'What!' he said. 'Natalie sent the clues? No way. I don't understand. Why would she? Why didn't she tell us when Star was missing? Why did she take you down into the cave? She must have known there wasn't any real treasure. I don't understand.'

'It was just a game,' I told him. 'She was just doing it for a laugh, you know, an adventure. That's all. But she fell. It was an accident. There was a chasm in the ground, and Natalie fell.'

I told him that Mark had saved the day, about how he'd been brave and calm, and Matt looked at me like maybe the bump on my head had done something to my brain and I didn't know what I was saying.

As we talked about what had happened, I told him there was one little thing that I didn't understand. Why had Natalie grabbed Shelly that night when we were looking at the stars? Was it just to make us all more jumpy?

'Oh, that . . .' Matt said, looking sheepish.

'What?' I asked him. 'You know something about that?'

'Yeah. That was me.'

'You grabbed Shelly? Why?'

'I wasn't aiming for Shelly,' he said. 'I was aiming for

Natalie. Not to grab her – to, you know, hug her. Because I fancied her.'

'Oh.'

If things had ended differently it would have been a funny story. But Natalie was dead, and telling the story just reminded us of that.

'I'm sorry, mate,' I said.

'Yeah.'

Even though I didn't want to talk to Matt about what had really happened with Natalie, I felt like I needed to talk it over with someone, and since the only person who could come close to understanding it all was Mark, it had to be him.

When we were alone in the infirmary, after the visitors had left and the nurse had brought us lunch, I broached the subject.

'When Natalie and I were in the cave together, before I found you,' I began, 'Natalie told me . . .'

'About her stepdad?' Mark cut across me. 'And her mum, in the boat?'

I was shocked into silence. 'How did you know?' I finally asked.

'I was following you,' he said. 'I heard.'

'Whoa,' I said.

'Yeah,' he agreed. 'Whoa.'

'I was useless,' I said. 'I just wanted to run away from her. But you were really good. You tried to help her. When she was threatening to jump, those things you said about her having a fresh start and not having to live up to the image she had of herself as being a bad person

– I think you were really getting somewhere. She was starting to come around.'

'Maybe. I don't know,' he said. 'It didn't feel like me talking, I kind of surprised myself. Normally I don't care about other people. Why should I? They don't care about me. It's just I could understand where she was coming from, you know? Like when my dad hits me, a part of me really wants to kill him.'

'But you don't,' I said.

'Of course not. You don't, do you? You don't go around killing people.'

'Natalie did.'

Yeah. Natalie did.

'Maybe she didn't really mean it,' Mark said, breaking the silence that had stretched out while we thought again about what Natalie had done. 'She was just a little kid when she did that boat thing – maybe she didn't think it would really happen. And then when it did, it messed with her mind. It's like there's this line that most people would never cross. But since she'd crossed it already, it wasn't there any more. It's like she thought she might as well keep killing people because she was already damned.'

I listened to Mark speaking. What he said made a lot of sense.

I was surprised at what an okay guy Mark was when he wasn't being all tough and bullying people. He said something about his dad hitting him. Don't they say that bullies often hit out as a form of self-defence – to attack before they could be attacked? I'd always thought

223

that that was just an excuse and that bullies were just jerks. Now I'm not so sure – people are a lot more complicated than I first thought.

'I think she could have changed, though,' Mark went on, and part of me wondered if he was really thinking about Natalie changing, or about himself. 'Why not? She didn't have to throw away her life because other people had been bad to her. She could choose to be her own person. She could choose to be a better person. It's not too late – I mean, it wasn't too late.'

I guess Mark was alone in the caves for a long time too. Maybe while I was singing nursery rhymes, he was thinking about deeper things.

Over the next few days I had to talk to the police and to Captain Bud. I told them bits of the story. I told them it had been a game – that Natalie had made a treasure hunt and we were pretending to be adventurers looking for buried treasure. I told them we'd got lost and separated and that Mark had somehow found himself on the other side of the chasm. I said that the rope had slipped when I'd been climbing over to him, and that Natalie had tried to save me but had fallen. I told them that I'd grabbed her wrists but that I hadn't been able to hold her. Apparently she had bruises on her wrists which backed up what I said – they were positioned like hands holding from above. There was no evidence that she had been pushed. Mark and I were not under suspicion.

There's not much more to tell. My mum and dad and Ryan arrived the next morning to travel home with me. I told them I could have travelled with the other kids, but they said that Captain Bud had paid for the flights, so they weren't about to turn down a free trip to New York. I guess he wanted to keep on their good side in case they decided to sue the camp.

I was kind of pleased to see them all the same, even Ryan.

'Cool scar, little bro,' he said, when he saw my face. 'Finally there's something about you that's not totally boring.'

I would normally have come back at him with some insult about his intelligence or something and it would have turned into a full-scale slanging match, but I didn't. I just laughed and said, 'Yeah, right.'

I don't expect Ryan and me to be best buddies from now on or anything, but at least I can start out trying to be more understanding.

Before we left camp, everyone exchanged phone numbers and e-mail addresses and promised to keep in touch. Matt lives quite close to me and he asked me to come and stay with him at the end of the summer. Ashley blushed when she gave me her address, and said she would write to me. I smiled at her and said I would write back. As we were leaving, Mrs Bud handed me a letter that had arrived at camp for me from Star. I slipped it into my bag to look at later.

We went to New York for the weekend before heading home – stayed in a hotel courtesy of Captain Bud, along with Mark and his mum. There was no sign of Mark's dad.

My parents weren't sure whether they should be walking on eggshells around me because of me being traumatised, but I was okay. Ryan and I climbed up the Statue of Liberty and we all walked around Central Park, and then met up with Mark and his mum for dinner in the hotel.

Natalie's body was sent home on the same plane as us. Her grandparents were too frail to come and escort it, so we took the responsibility. It was creepy to think of her lying in a coffin in the hold of the plane while we sat and watched the in-flight movies and ate the pre-packaged dinners. The rest of the campers didn't fly home on the same plane; they were due to leave a couple of days later. I guess it wasn't so easy to arrange a flight at short notice for so many kids.

I could see Mark and his mum having what looked like a pretty deep conversation in their seats a couple of rows in front of ours, and I hoped he was telling her about how his dad hitting him made him feel. I hoped that she would do something about it and that his life would get better. I suppose Natalie would tell me I was being overly optimistic, or naïve, but I still hoped I was right.

On the plane I took out Star's letter. I'd already read it in the hotel room, but I wanted to read it again. It was written before Natalie and Mark and I went into the cave, so Star hadn't known that Natalie was dead when she wrote it.

Dear Luke,

I was so dying to tell you all about 'my
ordeal' when you came to me in the infirmary and I wanted to scream at my mom
for making me leave so quickly. I feel
pretty dumb about going off after that
clue on my own. I suppose I was jealous
of you and Natalie and I wanted to keep
her out of it – you guys go back so far,
and she totally tries to dominate you. I
know you have this old clue-solving history
and everything together, and that really
ticks me off, but I'm sorry. I should
trust you enough to be happy about you
spending time with your old friend. I know
friends are important, and I don't expect
you to drop everyone else and be all
devoted to me or anything, so I'll back
off, okay?

I miss you so much. I know it's only
been like a day since I saw you, but I
feel like I'll die if I don't see you again
soon.

I've had all kinds of X-rays and things
and I've been stuck for blood tests
about a gazillion times – I'm getting an
insight into your world, hey?

It turns out I'm not that badly beat
up. I've got two broken ribs, but most of

the other injuries just look bad but aren't really. The doctors said that young people's bones are kind of bendy and less likely to break, but even so, they were amazed that I could have fallen as far as I did and not broken more bones, or ruptured my insides or something. I bet you're dying to know what happened, aren't you? Did I get attacked by wolves or bears, or set upon by Captain Bud with a meat cleaver? It was much more prosaic than that, I'm afraid.

I told the girls that I was sick so I could stay in the cabin and work out the clue. I was all determined that I was going to find the treasure on my own and show you and stinking stuck-up English Natalie (no offence) that us Americans aren't as stupid as you Brits like to think. So, when everyone was still in breakfast I crept to the hiking shed to get a rucksack then I hid while every-one was going to their first activities, before making my way around to the rope course. I had to be real careful beside the climbing wall, because there were people doing activities there. To cap it all I saw Natalie and her little mousy friend getting their harnesses on. I had

to duck behind the hedge that marks the
boundary of camp and sneak along the
outside of it, so I wouldn't be seen. I
wasn't looking where I was going, because
I was trying to see where the treasure
chest might be hidden, and someone must
have left some ropes lying around
because my feet got tangled up (for a
moment I thought someone had grabbed
my ankle and wrapped the rope around
it, but I must have imagined that bit,
huh? — or else what happened next
played havoc with my memory. Anyway, I
did this big klutz thing and fell all
over the place with the rope wrapped
around my foot, and I kind of toppled
into a hole . . .

The letter was very long. There were several pages
describing Star waiting in the cave, unable to walk
because she had sprained her ankles. She'd been terrified of not being rescued, of starving or dying of thirst
(she rationed out her water and trail mix – taking tiny
sips and nibbles only when she felt she really had to),
of someone coming down after her . . . I could only
imagine how awful that must have been. It was bad
enough just being in the cave for a couple of hours –
three days must have been a really long nightmare.

Eventually she signed off:

I hope you know how much it's hurting me to write this. Who knew broken ribs could be such a bitch? Even though they have me strapped up so much that I feel like I'm wearing a corset like a proper English lady, still just about everything except lying flat on my back hurts like Billy-o, and you know that I'm not the kind of gal that likes lying on her back. But for you, a bit of pain is worth it. I expect a nice long letter back from you. Let me know how the treasure hunt is going – I really want to know. I'm so bummed that I'm not there with all you guys. I guess I only have myself to blame, huh?

I really have to stop writing now and lie down before I pass out with pain.

I'll see you in my dreams,

Love

Star

I had to smile, reading Star's words. I could almost hear her voice in my head and see her animated face telling me how much she missed me. I knew I would have to write back, and that I would have to be honest with Star and tell her the whole truth, but I put off writing the letter until today. My therapist said that telling the story to Star would be good for me, to help me to get 'closure', and that working out how to say it in a letter would help me to organise the memories in my mind, which is a good thing, apparently.

I figured Star would probably have heard the official story of what happened at Camp Hope by the time she got my letter. It was bound to have been on the news in America – unless Captain Bud managed to hush it up again. But only Mark and I knew what really happened, and of all people I thought Star deserved to know the truth as well.

I wrote the letter this morning. It took up several pages of airmail paper, but still I was surprised that such a small thing could contain so much. I rehearsed what I was going to say over and over in my mind before I wrote it down, finding it difficult to put everything into words. I wanted to tell Star about what Natalie had been like before, when we were kids, and the terrible things that had happened to her to bring her to the point of madness. I wanted to convey the fear I felt in the cave and my confusion at Natalie's behaviour, and also Mark's role – turning my ideas of who was friend and who was foe completely on their head.

And most of all I wanted her to know that I was all right now, and that I hoped she was too. We'd both had a terrible experience, but it didn't have to change us for the worse. She could still grasp life with both hands, and maybe I could too. A lot of things had happened to me at Camp Hope, and yes, some of them were horrible, but some of them were fantastic, and most of *those* were thanks to her.

I remember back on the night of the camp-out in the

woods, someone said that the camp should be called Camp No Hope. At the time I thought, yeah, that was about right, but now, in spite of all I've been through, I can't agree. Camp Hope is a good name – because, after all, there's always hope.

- Acknowledgements -

Thank you to Charis McRoberts, who asked me one day if I would write about a treasure hunt (although I don't think The Trap is quite what she had in mind!).

Thank you to the Arts Council of Northern Ireland, whose generous grant made life a little easier for this 'penniless writer'.

Thank you to everyone at Faber, especially Julia Wells, who always makes my writing better, and Helena Zedig and Lucie Ewin.

And thanks always to my family – Paul, Becca, Daniel and Christy, just for being yourselves.